𝔇𝔯𝔶 𝔐𝔞𝔰𝔰

Joachim Ignatius Ryan, bachelor of
arts, doctor of philosophy pending,
centurion in the Legion of Mary, retired, takes up his first appointment in
a northern university. Here is a new
dish on the menu for the predators. For
although everyone in the Sociology
Department welcomes him, and some
even love him, he feels that there is no
communion, as in a dry mass.

Also by Joseph Martindale

FOUND WANTING

Dry Mass

Joseph Martindale

EYRE & SPOTTISWOODE · LONDON

01011098

First published 1969
Copyright © 1969 Joseph Martindale
Printed in Great Britain for
Eyre & Spottiswoode (Publishers) Ltd.,
11 New Fetter Lane, E.C.4 by
Cox & Wyman Ltd.,
Fakenham, Norfolk
413 44490 2

Contents

In a dry mass there is no Communion

For Alan Yeo, wherever he is

Introit

I

An old woman stumbled and fell, clumsily, on the dark stone platform, directly in front of Joachim's window. She lay there for a few seconds, unable or unwilling to summon the energy necessary to lift herself from the floor.

Joachim watched the people gather round her. None of them had noticed her as she shambled along the side of the train, every step drawing hard on her limited resources. None of them could have seen she was not going to make it to the carriage door. Now that she was prostrate on the cold stone she had become significant; something which drew people together in a small group, and encouraged conversation among strangers. A smear of red blood appeared on her forehead; it was clear that she was not going to be able to move without assistance. A man in a dark blue boiler suit bent over her to take hold of her arm, while the spectators murmured their concern. The old woman, dazed and embarrassed, dazed because she had hit her head on the stone floor, and embarrassed because no woman in her right mind would fall down, as she had done, in front of so many people, struggled breathlessly to her feet. Swaying slightly, she leaned heavily on the strong arm of the man in the boiler suit, while she made some feeble attempts to brush the dust from her clothes. The blood dribbled slowly from the cut on her forehead.

A woman in the crowd moved forward and wiped the blood away with a white handkerchief, to sounds of approval from the people on the platform and from the faces pressed against the windows of the compartment.

A smart little man, wearing the uniform of an official of British Rail, anxious to discover the cause of this interruption in routine, cut his way briskly through the crowd. He examined the old woman closely, took hold of her arm, and led her away to a crumbling wooden bench, where she sat down. The crowd moved into the train, glad that the woman had been seen by an official and that she would not be left to fend for herself.

The train vibrated violently for a few moments, shuddering forward. Joachim looked at the old woman, pale and shivering on the bench, officially declared unfit to travel. He pushed his tongue, irritably, into a hole in his tooth. He should not have eaten that packet of potato crisps; half of them seemed to have stuck in his tooth. Their sharp edges were needling his gums. It would not be long now before he would be forced to visit a dentist.

He had been on the train for four hours already and he had grown tired of reading. The week's political gossip lay strewn on his seat. He had read it all and he felt that he knew it for what it was: the tip of a murky iceberg, the bread and butter vomit of instant critics, none of them genuine prophets crying in a genuine wilderness. On top of this pile of magazines and newspapers was a modern paperback novel of indolent lust, which he had rejected after the third epigrammatic chapter. It lay, discarded, on the heap of magazines; the maiden on its cover, naked and demure, casting abused glances at the inhabitants of the long, stuffy compartment.

Another hour of the journey left and there was nothing to do. He looked at his fellow travellers to see if he could amuse himself at their expense. Most of them, well wrapped and coughing, were discussing the old woman who had collapsed at the previous station.

The jury, it seemed, was meeting to consider its verdict. Something unusual had happened and it was threatening the consciences of the people in the train. It had to be overcome. They dealt with it in the way mankind has dealt with the abnormal from the beginning. Events extraordinary are morally wrong and must be subject to moral condemnation. Where there is moral condemnation there must be a scapegoat to claim culpability and to take this with him into the wilderness so that the people can remain free from guilt. With a good deal of head-nodding and grunts of concurrence, the people in the train searched for a scapegoat.

Joachim heard the word 'disgusting' several times so he tried to work out what particular feature of the events on the platform had been disgusting. Perhaps the old woman was disgusting. But was she disgusting because she was old, or was she disgusting because she had collapsed? He listened hard but he could discover no details. Presumably, everything was disgusting.

The carriage door opened to admit a stocky man, wearing a dark overcoat and a yellow, silk scarf. He looked at Joachim's luggage, which was spreading itself out in the gangway. He then looked directly at Joachim and barked.

'You going all the way?'

'Yes,' replied Joachim, rather upset at the man's directness.

'Right. Well, you'll have to come and sit up here.' The man picked up one of the suitcases and made off with it up the train.

Joachim was very disturbed. As far as he had been able to ascertain, the man had not been wearing a uniform and had no right to go about the train picking up suitcases and telling their owners where they should and should not sit. Nevertheless, whether he had the right or not, the man had gone off with his suitcase and, if Joachim wished to regain possession of it, he had better do something about it.

Suppose the man was a thief. Joachim could not leave the rest of his luggage in case one of the man's accomplices came along and helped himself to it. Indeed, that might well be the plan.

Joachim acted immediately. Picking up his suitcase and his rucksack, he set off up the train in pursuit of the man in the yellow scarf. His luggage did not allow him to move as fast as he would have liked and it was some time before he caught up with the man who had taken his suitcase. He saw him disappearing into a small compartment. Joachim hurried along, arriving at the door of the compartment just in time to bump into the man, who was, it seemed, coming out to look for him.

'In here, son. There's a seat over there. You can put your luggage on the rack.'

Joachim went into the compartment and was amazed at the welcome he received. There were four other men in there, apart from the man in the scarf, and as soon as Joachim appeared they greeted him warmly, falling over each other to help with his luggage. It was not clear whether the five men knew each other or whether they had all met by accident in this compartment. In any case, there was such a display of open friendliness and bonhomie that he was taken by surprise. He sat down in the seat indicated by the man in the scarf, not really sure what to make of things.

There were six seats in the compartment and he found himself in the middle of one row, with his back to the engine and the man in the yellow scarf directly opposite him. The energetic conversation had not been allowed to falter since he had entered the compartment. Never had he heard the weather discussed with such enthusiasm; never had the discomforts and disadvantages of railway travel been subjected to such fiery bursts of analysis. From this Joachim deduced that the men in the compartment were strangers; had they been friends, their conversation would have centred on more particular topics. This made him feel more secure. He was, after all, surrounded by these men and the thought had occurred to him that they might have brought him here for some purpose.

'If you're going all the way you have to sit in this half of the train. The damn thing splits up half-way. They leave the other half behind,' said the man in the scarf, volunteering the first explanation of his behaviour. Joachim had forgotten his

anxiety about his suitcase and he received the explanation as
further proof that no one wished him any harm. He was still
fascinated by the difference in social atmosphere in this compartment compared to that which had prevailed in the one he
had left. There no one had said a word to him and his time had
been spent in comfortable isolation from his fellow men. Here,
whether he liked it or not, he was the centre of a conversation.
Indeed, there were moments when he felt that his travelling
companions were making an unnecessary fuss over him.

'I see,' he said to the man in the scarf. 'Thank you for telling
me.'

'That's all right, son.'

A short loud burst of unanimous laughter cut short any
conversation that might have continued from this. Joachim
looked at the other four men who seemed to be enjoying the
aftermath of a dirty joke.

'That was a good one.'

The cause of the laughter seemed to be the little man in the
corner. He was laughing along with the others but everyone
was looking at him and he was obviously rather pleased with
himself. Joachim thought it pitiful that little men should always
seek popularity in that way. 'Are you going hitch-hiking, son?'
It was the man in the scarf again. He must think that everyone
with a rucksack must be a hitch-hiker. If Joachim wanted to go
hitch-hiking he would not have started by taking a train.

'No. It's rather cold for hitch-hiking. I'm moving to a new
job.'

'What sort of job is it?' Old yellow scarf was very inquisi-
tive.

Everyone stopped talking and the compartment calmed while
Joachim spoke.

'It's at the university. I'm going there to do some research.'

'A student, are you?'

'No. I shall be known as a Research Fellow.'

'Research Fellow. That's a good name for a job.' Joachim thought he detected some disrespect in the remark, a suspicion which was strengthened when everyone started laughing.

'What is your subject then? What is this research all about?'

'Sociology. The university is introducing a programme of research into some new management problems. I shall be helping in this research.'

'Sociology. I thought that was helping the poor and meals on wheels and that sort of thing.'

'It used to be, about fifty years ago, when it was run by a man called Charles Booth.'

'I thought so. Didn't he start the Salvation Army?'

'No. That was General Booth, his uncle.'

The respect was returning now, and Joachim was making the most of it.

'You must be a clever boy to get a job like that.'

'Yes, I suppose I must be.'

There was a lull in the conversation while everyone looked at Joachim and worked out just how clever he would have to be to carry out his duties as a Research Fellow. The little man in the corner stuck his hands into his pockets and said that train journeys could be very boring. He would not mind so much if he was able to look forward to an interesting evening.

'Why, what are you doing this evening?' asked the man on Joachim's right.

'I have to go to the youth club championships and supervise some of the games.'

'What championships are these?'

'The national championships for all the kids in youth clubs. The finals are tonight. You know: table tennis, darts, bingo, and all that.'

'That should be quite interesting,' said Joachim, making conversation.

'Not when you have my job.'

'Why, what is your job?'

'I am in charge of the numbers.'

'The numbers.' Joachim did not know what he was talking about.

'Yes, the numbers. Have you never played it?'

'I have never even heard of the game.' Joachim shook his head.

The little man could not believe it. He looked round the compartment for support but no support was forthcoming. It seemed that none of the occupants had heard of this numbers game.

'Well. Blow me down! It's a card game; I'll show you.' The little man leaped to his feet, took off his overcoat and threw it on the rack, snatched his scarf, sat down again and wrapped the scarf around his knees to make a sort of table, all with such bewildering speed that Joachim thought he must have made it up. The little man produced a bundle of very battered, very marked playing cards from his pocket and began spreading them over his scarf. They were no ordinary playing cards these. There were about twenty of them, with their original surfaces defaced and large numbers pasted over them. As the little man explained the rules of his game, his hands moved very quickly over his scarf. Joachim watched him, without paying much attention to the explanation. The other men in the compartment watched with more interest but there was some evidence of suspicion on their part. Joachim felt a careful dig in his ribs.

'You want to be careful here, son,' whispered the man on his left confidentially. 'Keep your hands on your money.'

'Don't worry,' said Joachim. 'I never gamble on cards and this game looks far too complicated for me.'

The man with the cards saw that Joachim was not interested in what he was doing.

'It's a bit complicated if you have never played it before.

B

Shall we play another game? Come on; it will help to pass the time.'

Murmurs of disapproval could be heard in various parts of the compartment but nobody actually objected to the proposal so the little man carried on.

'What about Find the Lady?'

'I've seen that done before,' said the man on Joachim's left. 'I can find other ways of getting rid of my money without giving it away to cardsharps.'

'I'm not a cardsharp.' The little man was indignant. 'I just told you; I'm a youth club officer.'

Joachim had never heard the expression 'youth club officer'. As far as he knew, those men who worked in youth clubs were called leaders or wardens. The little man might well be a cardsharp.

'There's no need to talk like that,' intervened Yellow Scarf. 'If you don't want to play, don't play. There's no need to insult the man. It's a free country.'

The little man, grateful for this gesture of support, continued his sycophantic folly, fidgeting cleverly with the battered playing cards. 'Come on; it will help to pass the time.'

He selected three cards and began to distribute them over his scarf, his hands moving slowly and carefully. Everyone watched him. Joachim stared hard at the nimble hands, moving above and below each other in slow, careless arrogance, selecting a card here and tossing it there, without allowing any card to rest for more than a second. Suddenly the hands stopped moving and the three cards shuddered still on the scarf.

'Now,' said the little man, 'find the Lady.'

'Easy,' said the man on Joachim's right, who had concentrated very hard throughout the operation. 'The card on the left.'

The little man turned the cards over and the guess proved to be correct.

'I told you it was easy. Shall we make it more interesting?'

The little man looked nervously at the others. Joachim was aware of an elbow jerking into his left side.

'This is where the fool and his money are parted. If I were you I'd have nothing to do with it.' It was Joachim's self-appointed guardian angel again. Joachim looked at him, noticing, in passing, that the man's teeth were turning green.

'Don't worry. I've no intention of playing.'

'I'm game,' said the man who had just found the Lady.

'Well, we might as well do it properly. Who's going to hold the money?'

The little man jumped to his feet and fished several banknotes out of a small pocket at the front of his trousers. From this bundle he peeled two pounds, which he held above his head.

'Here's two pounds which says you will not find the Lady this time.'

'And here's two pounds which says I will,' said the man on Joachim's right who stood up, took several banknotes from the pocket at the front of his trousers, removed two pounds, replaced the bundle in his pocket, and sat down.

'Who's going to hold the money?' asked the little man again, while his eyes paid homage to those of the others, as they visited each in turn on a pilgrimage in honour of fair play.

'What about you, son?'

'Very well,' said Joachim, holding out his hand.

The four pound notes were thrust into his palm and he looked at them for some time before deciding what should be done with them. He could not sit there waving them about like paper handkerchiefs, he had been given a job to do and he must be seen to do the job properly. Fair play had a ritual and any neglect of ceremony might make nonsense of the whole project. He folded the pound notes carefully, rose to his feet, pushed the money into the pocket at the front of his trousers, patted the pocket with his empty palm and sat down again. He had always been interested in that little pocket. For some time he had remained convinced that its purpose was merely decorative and that it survived, like the buttons on the sleeve of his jacket, as a useless memory of a bygone fashion. But he had been very naïve. The pocket had been put there for a purpose and the purpose was now made clear to him. The pocket was there to hold money, money which had been pilfered very carefully from the other pockets in his suit and which was to be used for gambling. He fastened the button on his gambling pocket and sat back to watch the play.

'Are you ready?' the little man inquired of his opponent.

'Yes.'

The little man began to distribute the three cards over his scarf. His hands moved very slowly at first, so that it was fairly easy to follow the cards. But they did not move slowly for very long; Joachim watched, amazed and hypnotized, as the cards began to pick up speed. The cards vibrated terribly as they were seized, thrown down, seized again, thrown down, held, thrown down, one at a time, two at a time, and then all three at once were caught up in a whirlwind of frantic shuffling and juxtaposition. The moves were brilliantly conceived and perfectly executed. The nimble hands contrived, finally, to keep all the cards in the air at the same time, as they picked up a card here, made as if to put it down there, then, with the observers wickedly deceived, completely ignored it, while they concerned themselves with the other two. With the hands working at top speed, the man stopped instantly and the three cards gasped trembling on the silk scarf.

'My God!' ejaculated Joachim, breaking the shocked silence which followed the remarkable exhibition.

'Sh.' He was reprimanded by Yellow Scarf. He must have transgressed a point of ritual. The man on his right was concentrating very hard on the three cards. He breathed heavily through his nose for ages before he made up his mind.

'That one.' He pointed authoritatively at the card in the middle. The little man smiled quietly before he turned the card on its back. It was not the Lady.

'Hard luck.'

Joachim looked at the loser's face to see how the man was taking it. No trace of disappointment appeared; no evidence of sentiments of anger or of embarrassment. In fact there was no reaction at all: Joachim took the money from his pocket and gave it to the little man.

'Could have told you that would happen.' The man on Joachim's left did not seem to be addressing anyone in particular; his remark was in the nature of a general comment on the situation, an expression of opinion. The little man was most upset by it.

'What do you mean? Everything was fair and above board, wasn't it?' He looked for support to the man from whom he had just taken two pounds.

'I'm not grumbling. You beat me fair and square.' My goodness, thought Joachim, you are taking it well.

'I'll tell you what I'll do; I'll offer five to one. I can't make it fairer than that, can I?'

Joachim could not see how this gesture made the game more fair. If the man was cheating, the game was unfair, whatever the odds. But the little man, having made this offer, evidently thought that his integrity had been well established. The others thought so too.

'Seems very fair to me,' pronounced Yellow Scarf.

'I'll have a go at that price,' said the man on his right, standing up to fish his money from his gambling pocket. Joachim noticed that the elbow was prodding into his ribs again.

'Keep out of this, son.'

'Right,' agreed Joachim, wondering whether he should present the man with a signed declaration of non-involvement. He held out his hand to the parties to the game and received three notes; two for a pound and one for ten pounds. He examined the ten-pound note; this was only the second time he had ever seen a ten-pound note. He looked at the others who were unaware of his innocence. They all had fistfuls of money: notes for one, five, and ten pounds, which they were waving about like so many bus tickets.

The little man began to shuffle his cards. One of them fell on the floor but he picked it up quickly and made as if to continue. 'Better turn the cards over and start again. Then there can be no grumbling.' Yellow Scarf, who had taken it upon himself to referee this game, had obviously decided to eliminate any suspicion that the little man might have been up to something when he had dropped the card on the floor. The little man turned the cards over so that they were face-upwards and everyone could see that there was one Lady and two strangers. He picked them up, beginning that wonderful rhythmic movement of his hands in which he performed his magic on the cards. He proceeded more slowly this time so that Joachim was able to pick out the individual cards as they travelled over the scarf. He noticed that one of the cards had a bent corner and that it was easily separated from the others, even in flight. The cards stopped moving and lay back on the scarf. Joachim waited for the player to select his card.

'The one in the middle,' he said, pointing at the card with the broken corner. It was the Lady.

'Well done,' said Yellow Scarf.

'At least that should prove I'm not cheating,' observed the dealer.

'It certainly does,' replied Yellow Scarf, 'and we should give you a chance to get your money back.'

'Agreed,' said the man who had just won ten pounds.

The elbow was at it again. Joachim turned to face the man on his left, whose teeth were as green as ever and whose breath smelled of tobacco.

'Did you see the Lady? The corner is turned over. He must have done it when he dropped it on the floor.'

'Yes, I noticed it,' replied Joachim. 'I thought he must have done it on purpose.'

'Never. He hasn't even noticed it yet. You can spot it a mile off when you've seen it. I think I'll have a go this time.'

'I thought you said this game was for fools who wanted to lose their money,' Joachim observed, amused at the sudden disintegration of the man's principles at the prospect of easy money.

'Rubbish. This is money for jam. Never look a gift horse in the mouth. If I were you I'd have a fiver on it before he sees that bent corner.'

'Are you having a go this time, son? Come on: give the man a chance to get his money back.' This time it was Yellow Scarf. He was bending over and looking into Joachim's eyes, his own face, its tiny black spots varnished with after-shave lotion, only inches away.

'No thanks. I'll leave it to you. I never win when I gamble and I don't like losing.'

'All right, son, if that's the way you want it.' The man sat back in his seat. Joachim thought he detected an element of disapproval in his manner: somehow he was letting the side down.

'Never mind, I'll take you on.' The man on Joachim's left had forgotten his earlier misgivings. 'At five to one I think it's worth a fiver.'

'You're on,' said the little man and he began shuffling the cards over his scarf. He seemed to hurry his hands a little this time and no one bothered to hold the money. When the cards settled on the scarf the man on Joachim's left selected the one with the broken corner and won himself twenty-five pounds.

This time there was more pressure in the appeals to Joachim to participate in the game. The man on his left folded his

winnings, tucked them into his pocket and whispered that it
was money for jam and that Joachim was stupid not to take
advantage of the opportunity. The man in the yellow scarf leaned
over, almost threateningly.

'Come on, son. You can't sit there all day and do nothing.
This man has just lost thirty-five pounds, while you were sitting back enjoying it. You can't let him get off the train without
giving him a chance to get his money back.'

'Come on, lad. Don't be a wet blanket. You're not playing
with university students now.'

Joachim looked around him at the aggressive faces, ogling
him, urging him, blackmailing him, frightening him into pulling
out his wallet and joining their game. He was terrified by their
massive unity of purpose. It was a plot, a devilishly conceived
charade to take his money from him. My god, how stupid he
had been. It should have been so obvious from the beginning:
all that nonsense about express trains splitting up half-way
and the questions about hitch-hiking; all those suspicious half-
truths about youth clubs and the feigned interest in his welfare.
He felt bilious as he realized the exact nature of his predicament. He was alone in the compartment with five very clever
men, all of them eager to take his money from him. If they
chose to be violent, he would have no chance. Quite suddenly,
on a very ordinary train, in the middle of a very ordinary journey, life had taken one of its hysterical turns and he was in
danger.

He stood up and moved towards the door of the compartment. Nobody tried to stop him and this gave him courage. As
he heaved open the carriage door, he turned to face the enemy.

'I'm sorry, gentlemen, I'm afraid I never play your kind of
game.' This said, he leaped into the corridor, closing the door
quickly behind him.

The corridor was cooler than the compartment but it was
not cool enough for Joachim. His body was a million minute

fountains, with water coursing in slow double drops from the top of his neck through the shiver of his spine. He pressed his forehead on the cool window while his nervous hands searched his pockets for cigarettes and matches.

The train, meanwhile, moved on through the darkening night, picking its way through the jingle-jangle of moving rails with meticulous care. On each side, the telegraph wires rose and fell in a soothing circular motion.

The smoke from Joachim's cigarette filtered past the damp clot his forehead had left on the window. Once more he kicked himself for being a fool. His life at the university had been spent in the company of radical young men and women who had been content to divide the world into two distinct groups. These groups were variously defined but the relationship between them was always clear: it was one of exploitation. The first group were the rich, the overprivileged, the power élite, and they maintained their position at the expense of the other group, who were, in consequence, poor, underprivileged and impotent. On the basis of this analysis any social reform must be directed at the overprivileged state of the rich. Their propensity to exploit was seen to be a product of their economic and social position. Remove this position, eliminate this state of privilege, and there would be no vested interests to defend, no purpose in the rather distasteful exercise of cruelty towards one's fellow men. Utopia, naturally, had no social structure.

This diagnosis was naïve, but it was easily comprehended and formed the basis of such political agitation as his friends chose to inflict on the major social institutions of the period. In arriving at their conclusions they were careful to dismiss, sometimes arrogantly and sometimes with respect, depending on their source, any ideas or evidence which might have led them to sophisticate and perhaps modify their theory. If man's inhumanity to man is a product of his social situation then there can be no morality and the efforts at reform should be taken out of the hands of priests and given to sociologists.

Any ideas to the contrary were to be understood, like the lives of the poets or philosophers who produced them, within the context of the social situation in which they had been born. Thus, the ideas of the psalmist and of Aquinas and Hobbes were merely products of their different times, and very far from the truth. In any case, didn't Hobbes suffer from rheumatism or something? That couldn't have helped much.

Joachim pondered these great thoughts, sweating in the narrow corridor of the train as it leaped and shivered into the outskirts of the city. How clever and self-sufficient they had been! Completely outside the pale of most human enterprise, they had chosen to traffic in ideas which they had selected carefully and then built into a fortress. From this fortress, self-righteously guiltless, they had chosen to condemn the rest of the world. Supremely ignorant, they had formally deplored the lack of wisdom in others; intoxicated with theories of love, they had never recognized the exploitative nature of their own relationships. Painfully sensitive to the suffering of distant humanity, they had ignored the cannibalism of the hip tambourine men who had moved with the speed and silence of rats through the bohemian suburbs of the university.

Joachim had enjoyed his three years of cherry wine. He and his friends had dined and supped, talked and listened, laughed and played, loved and lost in three years of enthusiastic futility. It was only recently that he had begun to doubt. Only now, in fact, that he began to suspect that there was something in the nature of man which made him irredeemably carnivorous.

The train slowed as it neared the terminus. Joachim remembered that his luggage was still in the compartment with the five men. He did not relish the prospect of going back in there; those scoundrels would not be strangers to violence. If they decided to attack him there was nothing he could do to stop them. He turned round to look into the compartment; the men seemed very miserable. One of them saw him looking and responded by pulling a funny face which turned Joachim into a limp daffodil. He would have to wait until the five of them got off the train and hope that they had no designs on his luggage.

As the train pulled into the station he noticed a very tall man leaning against the door at the far end of the corridor. He was examining Joachim very carefully. Joachim thought he looked like an off-duty policeman.

'Anything wrong?' asked the man.

'I don't know yet,' replied Joachim.

'Do you need any help then?' asked the man, amiably trying another approach.

'If you could just stand here and look friendly. My luggage is still in there. Cardsharps. I refused to play. Moral support is all I need really.'

Joachim was not usually as inarticulate as this, but the large man seemed well able to act on ambiguous instructions.

'Right,' he said, taking up his position and regarding Joachim with a benevolent air.

Joachim, his courage returning with the presence of such a formidable bodyguard, looked again at the five men in the compartment. None of them had made a move towards his luggage; they were all seated, hands deep in the pockets of their overcoats, a very unhappy silent group. When the train stopped they stood up and followed each other out of the compartment, their hands still in their pockets and their shoulders bumping against the walls of the corridor. They ignored Joachim, who was left alone with the large man.

'Thanks very much,' said Joachim.

'No trouble then?'

'Apparently not. But there might have been if you had not been here.'

'Cardsharps, you said?'

'Yes. They were annoyed because I wouldn't play with them.'

'It takes all kinds.'

'Yes.'

'Well, I'll be off then.'

'Thanks very much.'

The man smiled, nodded, and then got off the train. Joachim went back into the compartment to pick up his luggage. He left the train just in time to see his erstwhile bodyguard disappearing past the ticket collector. The ticket collector was a man of the world. In his job he came across every known brand of human being; nothing could surprise him. Joachim came back to him after he had handed in his ticket.

'Can you see those five men over there?' he asked, pointing at the team who were waiting to board the train from which they had just alighted, evidently about to try to swindle someone else.

'Them?' replied the ticket collector, pausing from his duties to scratch his knee.

'Yes. They've just got off this train and they're getting back on to it again.' Joachim tried to make the matter seem urgent.

'Cardsharps. The police know all about them but they can't touch them. I'd have nothing to do with them if I were you.'

'Thanks for the warning.'

That was the end of the affair as far as the ticket collector was concerned. Joachim watched him close the barrier and clip the tickets of the five gamblers before they climbed back on to the train. He smouldered for a while, thought about explaining everything to the police so that the men would be caught and so prevented from preying on some other victim. But the prospect of explaining the events of the last hour in all their traumatic detail was too much for him. In any case, nothing had really happened.

He turned and made off into the city.

Gloria

I

Christine Murray, thoroughly healthy as a result of yet another camping holiday with her parents in northern Italy, had pressed the doorbell and was now summoning her sweetest smile to greet the landlady. At the end of the summer term she had written to Miss Deed at the University Accommodation Bureau, pointing out that she had been accepted for a postgraduate course and that, as she did not know the city very well, she might have difficulty finding accommodation. Miss Deed had replied by return, including the address of a landlady who had been on the university list for ten years and who was known to provide rooms of a very high standard. Christine was at this house now, waiting for the reputable landlady. The doorbell had already sounded, its four dulcet notes chiming sweetly behind the closed door, offering the visitor a clear picture of the bourgeois wealth within.

A shuffling of bolts and latches heralded the opening of the door. Christine smiled, but the door did not swing open as she had expected. A short, highly polished chain secured it to the joist and through the narrow aperture, which this allowed, a strong smell of furniture polish filtered into the open air.

'Who is it?' A woman's voice accompanied the exit of the furniture polish.

'Mrs Richards?'

'Yes.'

'Good afternoon. I'm Christine Murray. Miss Deed, at the University Accommodation Bureau, gave me your address. She said you might have a vacant flat.'

The door closed again while another bolt was lifted.

'Come in,' said Mrs Richards, now revealed as a stout, solemn woman in a pale, flowered housecoat. In her right hand she held a yellow duster.

'Thank you.' Christine stepped carefully over the marble doorstep and wiped her feet on the clean doormat. Mrs Richards closed the door, polishing the doorknob as she did so. A veritable house mouse, Mrs Richards.

'Have you no luggage?' she asked, unnecessarily.

'I left it at the station. I don't know this area very well. It's very heavy and I thought I could collect it later. I wasn't sure whether you would have a vacant flat.' Christine smiled again, but the charm that had warmed the heart of many a schoolmistress was wasted here.

'I always have a vacant flat when Miss Deed asks for one. She said you would probably write to me and confirm the arrangement.'

'I'm sorry; I'm afraid I spent the summer abroad.'

'It doesn't matter now; you're here and that's the main thing. Would you like to see the flat now?'

'Yes, please.' Christine smiled again, knowing no other technique.

Mrs Richards set off up the stairs, leaving behind a damp rubber plant and a pay-as-you-speak telephone, supplied by the G.P.O. She dusted the banister as she progressed. At the top of the house she paused before a locked door.

'This is your room. You have your own kitchen but you will have to share the bathroom with the two girls who live in the flat next to yours. They are both very nice girls and they always keep the bathroom clean.'

She took a bunch of keys from one of the many pockets in her floral housecoat and used one of them to open the door. Christine went in, ready to be impressed.

Every item in the room was spotless. Above the mantelpiece Holman Hunt's *Christ the Light of the World* looked down despairingly on the bric-à-brac below. His range of vision included a divan bed, tucked away in the corner farthest from the door, a small wardrobe with a gleaming mirror, three tiny rugs sailing on the polished linoleum, a single erect armchair and a coffee-table and stool. On every available surface rested a collection of vases, pots, candlesticks, porcelain dogs and ornaments of various shapes and sizes: the gravestones, it seemed, of many pleasant holidays at the seaside. There were no ashtrays but this was not likely to upset Christine, who was a healthy girl, not given to smoking. She liked men who smoked pipes but cigarettes were nasty, brutish and short. In her first year at the university she had refused to go out with any man who smoked cigarettes and, in consequence, her examination marks were the best in her year. But the course had become more difficult later and at the end of the third year she had to be content with a comfortable second. The only man in her year to prove himself worthy of a first-class degree had smoked thirty cigarettes a day.

'It's lovely,' she exclaimed exuberantly, turning to Mrs Richards.

'I try to keep everything nice and clean. When Miss Deed came round to see the house she said that if all her accommodation was like this she would be very happy.'

'I'm not surprised. It really is super,' said Christine, sincerely.

'Of course, it might not always be like this. After you have moved in it will be your responsibility to keep it clean. I try to go over everything twice a week but I can't always manage it. This is such a big house and it takes a lot of cleaning.'

'I can imagine.'

'I had a girl here once; I'm sure she must have been dragged out of the gutter. Every time I came in here her clothes were scattered all over the floor. She used to hang her smalls from the mantelpiece. Filthy girl. She never washed up. Used to leave dirty plates on the floor all night. It was a wonder the place was not full of mice. I had to ask her to leave.'

Mrs Richards paused, clasped her hands around her large middle and averted her eyes while she cut away the remaining tatters of the anonymous girl's reputation.

c

'And then there were the men she used to entertain. I have strict rules about men here. They have to be out of the house by eleven o'clock, which is late enough. I once caught a man leaving her room at eleven-thirty. That was the last straw. I wrote out a notice at once and pushed it under her door. She left the next day; without paying her rent, I might add. But I didn't mind that. I was glad to be rid of her. It took me two days to clean and disinfect the room after she had gone. Still, I expect you will be all right. You don't seem to be that kind of girl.'

'I hope not,' said Christine, looking innocent and hygienic, and then, with a touch of mischief: 'I'm very clean.'

'Your kitchen is next door and the bathroom is at the end of the landing. You should have all the crockery you need. If you ever break anything I hope you will tell me at once; some of the plates are difficult to replace and I like to keep complete sets of everything. Your rent will be four pounds ten and it is payable on Mondays. If you are going to pay cash could you please leave the money in your rent book and push it under my living-room door. I will return the rent book when I come up to clean your room. I have very few rules and I think I have mentioned most of them to you. The only thing I insist on is that all visitors should be out of the house by eleven o'clock. The rest I leave to the common sense of the tenants. Most of them have been very good so far. I'm sure you will too. There's no reason why you should not be happy here.'

Mrs Richards was, unwittingly, perfectly accurate when she said that Christine should be happy living in her new flat. Most people, faced with Mrs Richards's way of life and Mrs Richards's rules and regulations would have curled up and gone elsewhere. Not Christine. She had grown up with rules and regulations. For the last ten years she had spent most of her life carefully guarded by those rules and regulations supporting those institutions in which she had been educated.

At school she had learned how satisfying it was to win points for her expertise at bed-making – she had consistently held positions of responsibility in her dormitory and was everything her school matron could have wished for. From school she had gone to a northern university, where her literal observance of the rules and regulations in her hall of residence had won her the rare privilege of being allowed to stay there for the entire three years. Unlike some of her contemporaries, her room was always tidy and she never broke the curfew without permission. Other residents objected to the spasmodic visitations of the Bursar, who was reputed to burst into rooms without knocking, seeking what she could find. Christine welcomed these visits. As she never broke the rules she could never be found wanting. She loved being inspected. Now and then, the Bursar would call and Christine would offer her china tea, thus, in complete ignorance, providing the girls on the same corridor with valuable time to stop breaking the man-hour rules and to prepare for their own imminent inspections.

Mrs Richards would now replace the Bursar in the role of inspector, thus providing Christine with the same kind of motivation she had known for so long. Rules and Christine got on very well together; they needed each other.

'And whenever you go out would you please remember to close the door with your key. It saves the locks and it's much less noisy.'

'Of course,' said Christine, going out and remembering to close the door with her key. With the assurance of a child coming home from school, she pattered down to the bus-stop, where she caught a bus to the station and her luggage.

Joachim, having spent the night in a small, seedy hotel on the fringe of the city centre, was now engaged in seeking a more pleasant place to lay down his head. He had seen the notice board in the Students' Union and he had conversed with some of the local cognoscenti in the Union bar with the result that he now possessed some three or four addresses. There was no panic in his proceedings; he had plenty of time. More enterprising flat hunters waited in town for the first edition of the local evening paper which appeared on the pavements at lunchtime. More enterprising flat hunters had an incredible faith in the universality of the principle that the first come was always the first served. Joachim, being a sociologist, felt he knew more about the world than that. In any case, he was not looking for:

> Attractive, Self-contained Ground Floor Flat; hall, lounge/ living-room, kitchen, 2 bedrooms, bathroom, brick garage; £360 p.a. plus rates: unsuitable children. References.

He wanted a room.

The telephone in the kiosk was intact and operational. Joachim took out his list of addresses and dialled the first of the numbers. There was some clicking of wires and connections and eventually the noise of a telephone ringing at the other end. An interruption in the ringing indicated that the phone had been lifted. Joachim pressed his sixpence home.

'Hello, Mrs Davies?'

'This is Mrs Davies speaking.'

'Ah, Mrs Davies, my name is Ryan. I saw your advertisement in the Students' Union about your vacant room and I was wondering if it was still free.'

'Are you a student, Mr Ryan?'

'Not really, Mrs Davies. I have just taken a research post at the university which disqualifies me from calling myself a student. But I am not a lecturer either; I am neither one nor the other.'

'I see,' replied Mrs Davies, when the tone of her voice indicated that she did not see at all.

'Is the room still vacant?'

'Yes.'

'Could you tell me about it, please?'

'Yes. Well, it's a nice room and you will have your own wash-basin. It used to be my son's room before he died. This is the first time it will be used since then. My husband and I felt that the house was very quiet without him and we thought that, if we could find a nice young man who would appreciate it, we might not feel so lonely for him.' There was a pause and Joachim could hear the sounds of sniffling at the other end. 'Are you all right, Mrs Davies?' he asked, with some concern. He had already decided not to take the room. What the Davies were looking for was another son.

'Yes, thank you, Mr Ryan.'

'Would you prefer me to ring this evening and talk to your husband?'

'That is thoughtful of you, Mr Ryan. That would probably be best. I've never done this sort of thing before and I don't know what to say.'

'That is all right, Mrs Davies. Sorry to have troubled you.'

'Good-bye, Mr Ryan.'

Joachim put down the phone with some feelings of guilt. He had no intention of phoning the woman's husband later. He did not like telling lies or letting people down but there was surely no point in his involving himself in a situation like that one. He could have gone to live with the Davies and he could have played the role expected of him. This would have given them pleasure. But to do this he would have to live a lie. So, whatever he did, he was being dishonest. The world would not have it any other way.

He rang the next number and waited impatiently for the start of the next conversation.

'Hello. Is that Mrs Oak?'

'Yes.'

'Mrs Oak, my name is Ryan. I wonder whether you have a flat I might rent. I am new to the university but I heard that you sometimes rent flats to students.'

'Yes, that is true. Are you at the university, Mr er . . .'

'Ryan. Yes, I have just taken a job here.'

'Well, I do have a flat but it is not in this house. If you like, I could give you the address and you could go and have a look at it.'

'Just a minute. I will take it down.'

Mrs Oak dictated the address while Joachim transcribed it on to the back of an envelope. They arranged to meet outside the house twenty minutes later. Joachim left the telephone box feeling more at home. He felt safer when he dealt with a professional – the landlord–tenant relationship was, by its very nature, exploitative. Emotions got in the way here and could blind the parties to the real state of affairs. With a professional you could guarantee the minimum requirements of the Rent Acts and no more. Joachim wanted no more. A room and a landlady off the premises was what he sought and he had found it. He was, of course, very misguided to prejudge Mrs Oak and to categorize her so lightly. But then he was not clairvoyant and no one could expect him to do otherwise.

Joachim walked in the direction indicated on the back of his envelope, very impressed with the poverty of the environment and the wild, unclean aspect of the children. They teemed in hundreds in and out of cars and houses on his route, seemingly fearless but in fact very much afraid. Once or twice some of them were accompanied by a mother or an elder sister, but for the most part they were unattended; a savage, unkempt herd which had claimed the wilderness for its own.

And wilderness it certainly was. Originally the area had housed the middle classes in elegant Georgian terraces, three or four storeys high. Wide roads separated one row of houses from another and every two hundred yards the elegant houses paused to contemplate what had been the tasteful green oasis of a cultivated square. At the turn of the century these houses were in great demand for the sons and daughters of the merchant nobility, offering the security of expensive taste, and the delightful prospect of living with people of like kind. But the motor vehicle and the last war had changed all that. The rich moved farther out of the city and their former residences were bombed by an inconsiderate enemy. Bombed too were the jerry-built houses of the poor, which was more considerate of the enemy because the council needed the land. The poor had moved into the shells of houses vacated by the emigrant middle classes, bringing with them their children, their dogs, and their way of life, all of which were equally despised by the middle classes and by the social workers who were trying, in their own ways, to restore the *status quo*.

Joachim crossed through this waste land, picking his way carefully through the rubble and the vermin until he came upon the house in which he hoped to live. It stood aloof, separated by a bomb from the house next door and on the corner of a main bus route and what had been a very fashionable square. He stood at the corner, looking first at the house and then at the square, unable to work out which had made the greatest fall from grace. He was ten minutes early for his appointment.

While he waited he heard the noises of a disturbance across the road. There were children there, and the last time he had looked they had been busy throwing stones at each other and chasing one of their miserable dogs over the rubble. Suddenly they were very excited. They picked up clumps of wood and large stones, hunting some alien quarry. The dogs, too, were fierce and snarling. The children gathered in a circle, quietly moving into one corner of the bomb site. A rat, brown and heavy, scurried from the corner, squealing desperately for mercy. The children battered it with their weapons, piling blow upon blow and stone upon stone until the squealing ceased and there was nothing left but a mess of brown pulp and blood. This achieved, the children set off on a wild war dance, leaving the dead rat to the dogs. Joachim shuddered, remembering his adventure on the train.

Mrs Oak, when she appeared, surprised him. He did not think she was going to be so pretty or so well off. She drew up in a very large saloon car, which Joachim recognized as rare, and therefore expensive. She got out of the car and came over to him. She was not young but she was far from unattractive. Her figure, though ample, was firm and smooth and she wore the hair style of the generation which came after her, with some success. Joachim was pleased. From a scene of squalid death he was able to turn to a vision of life, because that was what Mrs Oak made him think about first. She generated life. She was, at the same time, maternal and seductive; a terrible prospect for someone like Joachim who had read Freud.

'Are you waiting for me?' she asked.

'Are you Mrs Oak?'

'Yes.' She tossed her hair as she spoke; a gesture, Joachim mused, which must have eaten the heart out of many a young man years ago.

'Then I am waiting for you.' Joachim bowed, amazed at how he was responding. He despised people who bowed before others.

'I'll show you the flat.'

She took him into the house and up the first flight of stairs, walking quickly and steadily on her high heels. She paused at the door of a room on the first floor, opened it quickly with a bunch of keys and went inside. Joachim followed her in.

The room was bigger than he had expected and had been divided into three separate areas by some clever work with hardboard screens. The living-room area was spacious, with a long couch, an armchair, a table, a chest of drawers and a tiled fireplace. There was also a small kitchen with a stove and sink and crockery enough for six. The other area was the sleeping space and it too had its appropriate furniture: a large bed, already made, a wardrobe and a dressing-table. Two large windows looked down from the living-room and bedroom on to the street below. Looking out, Joachim could see the deserted bomb site and the remains of the dead rat.

'How much is it?' he asked.

'Two pounds ten,' came the reply, surprising him.

'Then I'll take it.'

'At once?'

'Yes, my stuff is in a hotel down the road. I can get it now.'

Mrs Oak took out a virgin rent book and gave it to Joachim.

'You can pay me now if you like, or you can leave it till later. The bathroom is next door, your bed linen is changed every Saturday afternoon. My address is on the rent book so if you want anything you can get in touch.'

'I think I left my cheque book in my suitcase,' said Joachim.

'You can pay me tomorrow, then.'

'Right.'

Mrs Oak gathered her belongings and made as if to leave. Joachim watched her, puzzled by the low price of the room and by the very good service he thought he was going to receive for his rent.

'Mrs Oak,' he ventured, tentatively.

'Yes.' She had finished putting things into her handbag and stood looking at him, jingling her bunch of keys.

'I suppose you know you could ask much more for this room?'

'Could I?' she asked, knowing full well that she could.

'With the market in its present state, certainly.'

'I don't know anything about markets.' She picked up her bag and made for the door.

'But Mr Oak must know something about markets,' said Joachim, with no justification whatsoever, except to pry.

'There is no Mr Oak,' she said, opening the door. 'And no acorns.' Joachim smiled. The pun had been in his mind, but Mrs Oak had heard it too often before. She closed the door behind her and Joachim could hear her shoes clipping down the stairs. He went to the window to see her climb into her car. When she was out of sight he came away, looked once more at his room, testing the chair and the couch before leaving to collect his luggage and pick up sugar, milk and coffee.

At five o'clock on this clean and chilly September afternoon Mrs Ball returned from her afternoon at the Bingo Casino with a large envelope containing twenty-five pounds in cash. She parked her car outside the house in which Joachim had taken a flat, and went in. She had a flat on the ground floor – a living-room, a bedroom and a kitchen – in which she had been living for two years. She opened her living-room door, marched into the room, dumping her bag and her envelope on the table by the telephone. This done, she went into the kitchen to put on the kettle, eventually emerging from there to stand at the bottom of the stairs and shout at the top of her voice:

'Anybody in?' It was a terrifying scene. The woman, gaunt and haggard beyond her years, screaming harshly like that. The house trembled a little with the dissonant vibrations. The insane scream travelled up the many flights of stairs to be arrested at every carefully closed door *en route*. When there was no reply Mrs Ball returned to her kitchen and her kettle.

Joachim, meanwhile, had arrived at the front door with his luggage and was busy unloading it from a taxi. He paid the driver and went into the house. Half-way up the stairs he was arrested by a scream similar to the one he was fortunate not to have heard some seconds before.

'Where the hell do you think you're going?'

Joachim turned to see Mrs Ball, hands thrust down on her scrawny hips, feet apart in the manner of a television bobby, framed in the doorway.

'I'm going to my room,' he said coldly. 'I've just moved in.'

'Well you should have seen me first. I'm the caretaker here,' her tone was less harsh, but was still aggressive.

'I'm afraid I was not informed of your presence or of your function,' replied Joachim.

'Well, you know now,' replied Mrs Ball, unabashed. 'Go upstairs and put your bags away and then you can come and have a cup of tea.'

Not wishing to complicate his life with more hatred than was necessary, he dropped his luggage in his room and returned, as instructed, for the cup of tea.

'I am Mrs Ball and I am the caretaker here,' said the woman, leaving him to go back into her kitchen. Her exit did not prevent her from making an attempt to continue the conversation; while she made the tea she directed shout after shout at Joachim, who could not make out a word she was saying.

Her living-room was a mess. The fire had not been laid properly for days and it was a heap of ash, cinders and cigarette packets. The mantelpiece was a jungle of postcards, candlesticks, clocks, ashtrays and photographs, all paying dusty deference to a large mirror and a portrait of the Queen. Each unfortunate article of furniture was buried in newspapers, paper bags, bits of electrical wire, torn lampshades and dust. The table in the window wore yesterday's dirty dishes on a green cloth which had been thrown carelessly over its surface. Above the piano a large, six-armed plaster woman had been plugged into the wall; she held a light bulb in each hand and at the flick of a switch she could double the illumination in the room. Joachim could see her through the mirror above the mantelpiece. The only item which was not buried in dust or delft was the telephone, which shone, black and strong, on the table by the window. Everything else was obviously ashamed; the carpet, having seen better days, took every opportunity to run and bury itself under the couch.

'Are you deaf or something?' Mrs Ball had come back into the room with a tray and the tea things.

'I don't think so,' replied Joachim, growing accustomed to her manner. 'Why?'

'I've been talking to you for the past five minutes, that's why.'

'I couldn't hear you.'

'Well, you should have told me. I haven't got breath to waste. Have some tea.'

'Thank you.' Joachim took the cup from her. As he drank, a soggy tea-bag on a piece of string settled on his tongue. He spat it out quickly into his saucer.

'I thought you were supposed to put those in the teapot.'

'It doesn't matter whether you put them in the teapot or in the cup. It says so on the packet. What's your name?'

'Ryan. Joachim Ryan.'

'That's a funny name. Hey, are you a Jew?'

'No.'

'It's a Jewish name though.'

'Ryan isn't.'

'My name is Mrs Ball. My friends call me Vicky.'

'You have friends,' said Joachim sarcastically, still suffering from the tea.

''Course I've got friends, hundreds of them. You can call me Vicky since you live here.'

'Thanks, Vicky.'

'Had your tea?'

'No. I'll get something in town. I haven't had time to stock up yet.'

'Stay where you are. I've got enough for both of us.' She

jumped up from her chair and went once more into the kitchen, coming back with half a cold chicken which she dumped on the table. Joachim could not make this woman out. She changed from Dr Jekyll to Mr Hyde with the speed of light, and for no apparent motive.

'Eat this, it will do you good.' She gave him a leg of chicken and a bottle of pickled onions.

'What about Mr Ball? What will he eat?'

'There is no Mr Ball. I divorced the bastard ten years ago.'

'This area seems remarkable for the number of its absent husbands.'

'He was no husband; he was a bastard.'

'So you said.'

At this point Vicky became excited, dramatic and very conscious of her personal experiences as an abused woman. She told Joachim the long history of her relationship with her husband; and how he had been a seaman and of how he had accused her of running around with other men, she who was bearing his child. One evening, he returned from sea while she was out at the chip-shop and he had attacked her when she returned, accusing her of infidelity. This kind of behaviour on his part, together with the death of her daughter, eventually convinced Vicky that their marital relationship left much to be desired and one day she had deserted him, a fact which did not prevent her from divorcing him later on the grounds of cruelty. The language used by Vicky, when she told this story, was expressive, colourful, and indelicate. Joachim asked her many questions and warmed to her as her narrative plunged farther into the realms of fantasy. Outside, the air grew dark and cold as afternoon made way for evening and evening for night. Vicky continued her narrative, struggling hard with her imagination to evoke horror after horror. She was interrupted, finally, by the telephone.

'You will have to go now,' she said, after she had finished

with the phone. 'A friend of mine is coming round to see me, a boy-friend.'

'Well, I'll leave you to it,' said Joachim. 'Thanks for the tea and everything.'

'Don't forget that I'm the caretaker here. If you break the rules you'll have to answer to me.'

'I shall live in fear and trembling at the imminence of your wrath.'

'And close the door; this isn't a bloody field!'

Joachim closed the door and went up to his room, where he unpacked his luggage. When he had finished it was late and dark. It was not late enough for all the children to have disappeared – he could see them gathered at the door of a pub some way off, receiving crisps and nuts from an unseen hand at the other side of the door. Vicky's friend came, but he did not stay very long. He was replaced by another and then another, events which Joachim did not consider significant until he saw the last one leave, just before he went to bed.

'My God,' he said out loud, 'she's a prostitute.'

Outside, the scene was suddenly desolate of children; the pubs had closed and their parents had taken them home. All that remained were several quiet cars, cruising slowly at the edge of the pavements, the flickering of a Belisha beacon somewhere down the road, and the occasional footsteps of someone going home.

Down on the bomb site a scavenging dog sniffed excitedly around the remains of the brown rat.

2

A fine, slow mist of rain had settled on the city during the night, darkening the dust on the windows without washing any of it away. Joachim had slept well and long, amused at the busy rustlings of a mouse somewhere in the kitchen quarters of his flat. He lay on his back, hands tucked underneath his head, remembering the mouse in the chaplain's dining-room at school. The chaplain, a very old, very lonely priest, used to eat alone four times a day, except on feast days and when he was away at the races. For three months Joachim had brought him his meals four times a day, to be instructed on each visit in the popular idioms of the French language and in the horrors of trench life during the First World War. In one corner of the dining-room was a mousehole and Joachim and the chaplain would take it in turns to leave a slice of fresh brown bread in front of the hole every evening. The chaplain was very fond of his mouse; he could never accept the fact that it was afraid of him. Joachim often found him on his knees in front of the hole, trying to woo the creature out. The mouse was a secret, known only to Joachim and the chaplain until one day when the Bursar was measuring the dining-room for a new carpet which the chaplain did not want, he found the mousehole and promptly filled it with rat poison. The Bursar, understanding the loneliness of the old priest no more than he understood the loneliness of the boys in his charge, did not notice the chaplain's subsequent depression and decline and was, therefore, very surprised when the old man died in his bed a month later.

For his part Joachim was pleased to share his room with a mouse. Gregarious by nature, he welcomed the companionship. If his religion forbade the presence of a woman in his bedroom, there was nothing, so far as he knew, in Canon Law about mice. He got out of bed to put a biscuit in front of the mousehole in the kitchen, in memory of the old priest.

In keeping with the liberal human relations policy for which universities are so famous, Joachim had been asked to present himself at the Department of Sociology and Social Administration 'sometime in the morning'. He set off across the sunlit wilderness, having ascertained that Vicky was still in bed, though whether at work or at rest he could not tell. She could hardly be sleeping because the house was full of the screams and shouts of children bursting the seams of the basement flat. The wilderness, with its swirling dust was quiet at this time of day, though this did nothing to improve it.

The university had settled on the city in the same way that water finds its way on to a shaving mirror. The policy of the administrators, as stated in the Staff Handbook was to 'retain the best of the old while, at the same time, leaving the way open to exploration and experimentation in the adventurous use of current architectural techniques'. Joachim, having seen the buildings and having read the handbook, was sure that the handbook had been put together in the School of Architecture and the new buildings designed in the English department. As he approached the Department of Sociology and Social Administration, which he was glad to observe was contained in what remained of 'the best of the old', he was able to see how the university was spreading through the poor areas on its borders. Here and there a small shop fluttered its beaten wings as it waited for the death blow. All around, bulldozers and cranes were mercilessly tearing down old buildings, uprooting whole communities of people and networks of relationships, preparing the ground for the construction of fine new offices in which clever men could talk to each other self-righteously, and from positions of knowledge and experience, about Town Planning, Juvenile Delinquency and the Democratic Regulation of the Price of Land. The occupants of the demolished houses had been moved out to housing estates, which they hated, while the university threw up more buildings for thinking about, discussing, and setting in motion the construction of more housing estates. The university was spreading through the city like a bubbling oil spring, devouring and defiling everything in its path.

Joachim went into the old building through the two majestic double doors which gave access to a large oak-panelled entrance hall. A somnambulant porter nodded at him as he passed. Strangers presented no threat to the porter's serenity, his main enemies being students and noise, phenomena which had the habit of arriving simultaneously.

The entrance hall was dominated by a large fireplace which waited, open-mouthed and fierce, like a bulldog crossed in love, ready to devour anyone who did not treat it with the respect it felt it deserved. It was an educated fireplace, designed in the grand manner, and not in the least ashamed of having been chosen to decorate one of the lesser departments in the university. Most of its stones were carved with stories from the Greek and Roman legends – Icarus falling from the sky, the Minotaur and Theseus, Aeneas with Cerberus and good solid stuff like that. It was not out of place in the Department of Sociology and Social Administration which spent most of its time in the perpetration of mythology, albeit with reference to the contemporary scene.

At each end of the room, symmetrically placed and equidistant from the fireplace, two small staircases rose quickly from the floor and scampered in short circular steps up into the mysterious corridors and rooms above. One staircase was marked 'UP' with an arrow pointing in that direction for the benefit of foreigners and illiterates, while the other staircase was marked 'DOWN' with another arrow pointing to the floor. The brain behind this elementary form of traffic control was the Professor of Social Administration and many members of

D

his staff believed that this achievement alone was sufficient to justify his appointment to his chairs.

But traffic control was not the only purpose of the notices. The Professor of Social Administration, like all eminent academics, was plagued with visitors from all sorts of organizations, some sensible, some daft. His office was positioned on the second floor, at the point where the two staircases met momentarily before shooting off into the upper reaches of the building. When the professor was threatened with a visitor he would leave his room and take the 'DOWN' staircase to the ground floor, leaving the visitor to be detained by his secretary until he contacted her by means of the porter's telephone in the entrance hall. If the visitor was genuine, the professor returned to his room at once, going back up the stairs marked 'DOWN'. But, if the visitor was suspect, the professor's evasion plan was put into operation. This was set off by the secretary, who would inform the visitor that the professor had just gone downstairs to look for him. The visitor would take the 'DOWN' stairs while the professor returned to his room via the 'UP' stairs. When the visitor reached the entrance hall, the porter would tell him that the professor had gone back upstairs. This deceit would continue, with the professor back in his room, the secretary directing the visitor down and the porter directing the visitor up, until the poor man tired of running round in circles and went home. This whole operation relied heavily on the discretion of the secretary and it was not until the day when she refused to admit the professor's wife that he became aware of the extent to which he had abdicated real power.

To add to the confusion of strangers, a third staircase, with neither notice nor arrow to clarify its destination, stood, well worn, at the end of the room farthest from the door. This led to the students' lavatories and to their common room, where they carried out their extra-curricular activities, safe from the terrors of the proctor.

Joachim set off up the stairs marked 'UP' and bumped into a confused Christine Murray who was coming down. She was pretty so Joachim smiled. She looked at him and stopped, obviously disturbed.

'Is anything wrong?' asked Joachim, sympathetically.

'Are these the "UP" stairs or the "DOWN" stairs?' she asked, by way of reply.

'I think these are the "UP" stairs,' said Joachim, 'but I don't think it matters all that much. There's no dragon on guard at the bottom.'

'Perhaps not, but I don't want to get off to a bad start.'

'Well the "DOWN" stairs are over there,' said Joachim, who had been here before for his interview.

'Are they? Thank you very much.' Christine Murray smiled at him and walked away. Joachim watched her, very taken with her innocence.

His journey took him past the office of Professor Padd, the Professor of Social Administration. Outside it sat three clean young men listening to a conversation between the professor and another clean young man. Joachim heard a snatch of the conversation as he passed.

'But I haven't been interviewed yet, Professor.'

'What is your name?'

'Morgan, Professor.'

'Morgan . . . You have been interviewed. Morgan's name has been ticked off on my list.' The professor waved a sheet of paper in front of the young man's eyes.

'But I have been sitting here all morning. I should know whether I have been interviewed or not . . .'

'Everyone has been interviewed. The interviewing panel has gone to lunch. Look: six names, six ticks. A very tidy operation.'

'But I've come all the way from Cardiff.'

'You should have stayed at home. You are much too young

for the job, as I told you during your interview. In any case, we never employ Welshmen; we find them a very unintelligent race.'

Joachim passed on, grateful that he was not working with the social administrators. The young man from Cardiff collected his expenses from the secretary and went back home. Three months later he fell off a mountain, an event considered sufficient to qualify him for a job with the Adventure department of B.B.C. Wales.

The door was open, so Joachim looked inside before he knocked. Quentin Tumble, the *enfant terrible* of British sociology, was throwing letters all over the floor. A dozen envelopes flashed through the cigar smoke before scuttling across the polished linoleum.

'Come in.'

Joachim went in; the man had disappeared.

'Ah, good morning, Ryan. Sit down and put your feet up.'

The voice came from a filing cabinet behind the desk. Joachim was not surprised. Quentin Tumble had once arrived at a conference of the British Sociological Association in the full dress of a piper of the Black Watch for no other reason than to give visual aid to a lecture on 'Bundling and military recruitment in the Shetlands'.

'There it is.' He rose from the floor, blushing with the effort. 'It was hiding under the filing cabinet.' He held up the letter so that Joachim could see it before he tossed it into the air.

'Expect you're wondering what I'm doing.'

'You are throwing letters on the floor.' Joachim watched it settle near his feet.

'It's my system. If I leave them on my desk I forget to post them. If they are all over the floor I can't possibly ignore them. Can I?'

'What about your secretary?'

'Haven't got one. Can't have one. Padd's economizing on secretaries. Have to use those things.'

He pointed at a dictaphone on top of the filing cabinet. Next to it stood a curious sculpture made from string and knitting needles. It was labelled 'Model: Social System'.

'Want some coffee?'

'Please.'

'We'll have to go upstairs. Then you can go home if you like. There's nothing for you to do yet. Project meeting on Thursday at eleven. Pick these up and post them on your way out, will you?'

Quentin Tumble was Joachim's boss.

Christine Murray went down the 'DOWN' stairs, smiled at the porter and pattered busily out of the building. First she must go to the bank to arrange to have six pounds a week transferred from her branch in Surbiton. Then she ought to buy a bus-timetable and some china tea. Mrs Richards was due to clean her room this afternoon and she wanted to catch her. There was nothing to clean – Christine had seen to that the previous evening. Mrs Richards would be delighted beyond endurance to see her work done for her and then to be offered china tea. It was in this way that Christine seduced her elders.

Tomorrow she must buy some books. Her reading list included several paperbacks which she could easily afford. She would start with *Child Care and the growth of Love* and *Invitation to Sociology* and go on from there. She would never be able to buy some of the others. She would have to borrow *The Social Services of Modern England* from the library until she could persuade her father to send her a copy. Some books on the reading list had the most terrifying titles. *The Tennessee Valley Authority and the Grass Roots* for instance, sounded more like a book on methods of irrigation than suitable literature for someone preparing to become a Child Care officer. Still, she would have to read it, along with all the others.

Not today though. She was going to surprise Mrs Richards today with china tea and Scottish shortbread. Academic pursuits could wait until the morrow. Lectures did not begin until next week.

She bought her various articles at the appropriate shops, took a bus home. A note had been pushed under the door of her room.

Dear Miss Murray,

I shall not be able to clean your room today. My sister has been taken ill in hospital. If any foreign salesmen come to the door please ignore them. If you don't they keep coming back.

Elizabeth Richards.

'Bother,' said Christine, her afternoon's work destroyed before it started. She would have to think of something else to do. She could start by having a cup of tea alone, then she could take a bath. In the evening she might be able to persuade one of the girls next door to go with her to the cinema. Outside, it had begun to rain, harshly turning the slow afternoon sour and miserable. Christine looked out of the window for a few minutes. Then she came back to her senses and walked quickly into the kitchen to put on the kettle.

Far from being lonely, Joachim was suffering from a surfeit of strangers. At coffee he met a curious mixture of sociologists, some of them academics, some of them eccentrics, like Quentin Tumble; others saints in sinners' clothing, who wandered through the common room scattering responsible morality among their brethren with the same viciousness found in some people who throw rice at weddings. One of these mendicant friars cornered Joachim as soon as he received his coffee.

'Morning. Ryan, isn't it?' He held out a bony hand, brown with nicotine.

'Yes.'

'Pretty, Charles. Moral Philosophy. Welcome to the hot-house.'

'How do you do. Thank you very much,' said Joachim, taking things in chronological order.

'What is your position?'

'Research Assistant to Quentin Tumble.'

Charles Pretty laughed. His long frame shook inarticulately, the convulsions eventually travelling to his coffee cup which overturned and sent its contents running down the man's suit.

'I didn't mean that. I meant your philosophical position.'

'I don't think I have one.'

'Good. You have an open mind. I thought you might be a Logical Positivist. At least I thought you might think you were a Logical Positivist. No one can be a Logical Positivist because Logical Positivism is a spurious game.'

'I'm not a Logical Positivist.'

'What are you?'

'I'm not anything.'

'Good. Not being anything is quite different from being nothing. I'm glad you appreciate the difference.' The coffee dripped steadily from his jacket. He ignored it as he proceeded.

'Have you any religion?' He said this as though he were talking about cigarettes.

'I'm a maladjusted Catholic,' replied Joachim, unconsciously talking in labels.

'Very good. Why are you maladjusted?'

'Because I grew up in a Church which formed me and I now see that this Church is in a mess.' What a crazy conversation this was.

'What do you mean by mess?'

'The Church no longer propagates good, at least not totally. It sometimes perpetrates evil.'

'You're a Pragmatist.'

'No. The Church is a Pragmatist. That is what is wrong with her.'

'I see. We must continue this conversation on some other occasion. I have to dash now. A class of young Marxists. Very stimulating.'

Charles Pretty dashed off, coffee dripping from his jacket, eager to spend another hour sticking labels on to the minds of his students. Joachim was glad to see him go.

'I see Charles has been after you already.' Quentin Tumble was back, his yellow shirt splattered with spots of coffee.

'He was interested in my position.' Joachim was already growing sarcastic.

'He would be. I came over to tell you that your room is on the top floor. There are three other men in there with you. You can't miss it; your name is on the door. You won't forget to post those letters, will you? I must get back to work.' Quentin Tumble was off in the wake of Charles Pretty, leaving Joachim stranded in the corner of the large coffee-room, at the mercy of a score of unknown assorted academics.

As he watched the performance from his corner Joachim was reminded of Gerald Scarfe's many portraits of the House of Commons in the full vigour of its pantomime. There were rituals here too. People entered the room prepared for combat, ready to do battle with wit, anecdote, dress and deference to secure positions in the pecking order. People conformed and knew it, rebelled and knew it, stood on the sidelines and watched and knew it. The savage game was subject to very strict controls; a species of academic Queensberry rules which kept outsiders away and allowed the combatants to destroy each other respectably in the name of academic freedom. Absent members were ridiculed, old jokes revived, laughter forced, petticoats revealed, as each combatant fought for the attention of the assembly and, in so doing, for its domination. There were no mirrors in the room so that the only image of oneself was to be seen in the reactions of one's fellows. These reactions were sure to be as false as one's own behaviour, subject as they were to the same forces of self-interest.

To Joachim, a temporary outsider, the whole display was a nonsense and bore no relation to anything that was worthwhile. He picked up his pile of letters and escaped. He would have to pay tribute to the herd soon enough.

He left the room and the building, going out into the rain which had just begun to fall softly. A bus paused outside the door of the department to deposit two students. Joachim saw that it was going past his flat so he jumped on.

'First one only,' commanded the bus conductor with some wit. The bus was empty except for Joachim. He got off outside his flat with the rain, heavy now, driving hard into the mud on the deserted bomb site. Vicky was out, the house dark and silent, his flat cool and claustrophobic. He lit a fire, made some coffee, smoked a cigarette, read two more chapters of the paperback novel and eventually fell asleep.

The rain fell heavily throughout the afternoon. Christine Murray watched it from her bath as it battered against the bathroom window. She should have felt comfortable and secure, safely locked in the scented hot water, but the disappointment of Mrs Richards's departure had left her depressed. Vicky had won again at Bingo. The rain tippled on top of her as she got out of the car and ran into the house. Unlike Christine, Vicky was elated. 'Wake up, you lazy bugger. We're going to the pictures.'

She had a key to Joachim's room which she had entered in the manner of an impertinent jailer. Joachim woke up to see her standing in front of the fire. She was holding a brown envelope in one hand while she scratched her bottom with the other.

'Hello, Vicky.' Joachim stood up to rub his right leg, which had not woken up with the rest of him. The fire had almost gone out but the room was still very warm, in spite of the sharp draught of cold air which was hurtling in through the open door. 'I didn't hear you come in.'

'You must have a good job.' Vicky felt that she was at her best; good humoured, aggressive and vulgar, playing with Joachim as a lioness plays with her cubs.

'What's up with your leg?'

Joachim stopped rubbing his leg. He walked to the door and closed it. Perhaps, if he were very polite to Vicky, she might go away.

'Would you like some tea, Vicky?'

'No. I told you we're going to the pictures. Go and get a paper.'

'A paper?' Joachim was not yet fully awake.

'Yes, you bloody fool, a paper, a paper. We can't go to the pictures until we know what's on, can we?'

Vicky said this with scorn, feet still astride, one hand on her bottom, the other beating time to the rhythm of her words. The brown envelope rose and fell in front of her in perfect time until she reached the end of her statement. Both the envelope and her voice recognized the end as clumsy. She finished on a high note, the envelope struggling in mid-air, like a kite pulling on a string.

'It's a bit early for the pictures, isn't it, Vicky?' said Joachim feebly.

'I always go to the first house. I don't like being out in the dark.'

Joachim, a little quicker by now, recognized the wisdom in her statement. If Vicky were to stay out too late she would disappoint her clients. How could they reach her if she were in the cinema? Vicky's position must be insecure enough: with her declining looks and charm she could not have many years left in her profession. How many clients must have left already, tempted by the fresher, if less experienced, talents of a younger generation of prostitutes? Vicky could not afford to alienate any more. If she was no longer beautiful she must, at least, always be there when her clients needed her. Availability was her sole asset. 'Right, Vicky, I'll go out for a paper.' Joachim had nothing else to do that evening. If Vicky wanted him to go to the pictures then he might as well go. His mother had always told him that he was too easily led and that he had no mind of his own. This was not strictly true. It was just that he found it more convenient not to disappoint other people. It was rare that he found it impossible to reconcile his own immediate wishes with those of others. He rarely had immediate wishes.

He returned with the newspaper to find Vicky in her kitchen making a pot of tea. She wanted to see a Western or a love story so Joachim suggested that they should try 'Cat Ballou' which was revisiting a suburban cinema. After they had finished their tea in her sitting-room they set off in her car.

She drove, as she behaved generally, with no regard for the conventions and with a royal disdain of the needs and wishes of her fellow motorists. Fortunately, they came short of actual collision but she found occasion to stop the car three times to shout abuse through the window: twice at timid cyclists who dared to be on the same road as herself and once at a young Negro who had ventured on to a zebra crossing as she approached it. This man she managed to insult without referring to the colour of his skin, a feat Joachim thought remarkable. Here, apparently, was a woman without prejudice; she either loved everybody or hated everybody, as the occasion demanded.

'Why did you suddenly decide to go to the pictures?' he asked, in a pause between hostilities.

'Won again.' She fished out the brown envelope from under the dashboard and handed it to him. He read the greeting printed on the front.

CONGRATULATIONS on your well-deserved win. I hope you will come back again.

S. Whitfield-Jones,
Director, Locarno Casino.

'How much did you win?'

'Twenty-five.' Vicky spared her passengers the minimum of words when she was busy at the wheel.

'Do you win often?'

'Twice a week.'

'Really.' In the face of such fierce brevity of temper Joachim was reduced to talking like a man from the B.B.C.

'We're here.'

So they were. The cinema was upon them suddenly. Vicky braked and turned into the car park, scattering three children and a dog who were walking across the entrance. Behind her there was panic as several drivers stamped hard on their brakes; she had pulled into the car park, as usual, without giving a signal.

'Mind your car, mister?' A small boy with a very dirty face and a hole in his shirt, approached Vicky as she got out of the driving seat. He had obviously been outdoors for some time: his clothes were very wet and his hair was lying flat on his head as if someone had recently run over it with a hot iron.

'Bugger off,' said Vicky, contemptuous of his poverty and of his innocence.

Unperturbed, the urchin came over to Joachim.

'Mind your car, mister?'

'How much?' asked Joachim, feeling for some change.

'Shillin',' replied the boy, candid and unafraid.

'What's your name?' Joachim gave the boy a shilling.

'Robertowen.' The boy took the shilling and began to polish one of the headlights with the sleeve of his jacket.

'Look after it well, Robert Owen. Guard it with your life.'

'Come on. We'll be here all night.' Vicky was impatient. Joachim followed her round the corner into the foyer where she bought tickets and then joined a small queue at the popcorn stall. He would have preferred to have bought the tickets himself but he was not going to challenge Vicky about that here. Instead, he went outside to look at the car and its sentry. Robert Owen's body was rigid, his face set hard and firm. He was obviously prepared to lose life and limb defending his charge against whatever enemy fate might care to send him. Joachim chuckled and returned to the foyer to find Vicky engaged in a fierce argument with the girl behind the sweet counter. A small, predatory crowd was watching her, much amused.

'I gave you half a crown, you cheeky little bitch.'

'No, madam; you gave me two shillings. Here it is. You owe me another sixpence.'

Joachim intervened quickly, slapping sixpence on the counter and leading a protesting Vicky away by the arm. She grumbled all the way to their seats, while, around her, members of the general public were openly disgusted at the language she used. They said so, one to another, in whispered conversations. When the lights dimmed they sat back in their seats, glad they had been given a real opportunity to cast a few stones. Joachim could feel them patting themselves on the back in an orgy of self-congratulation.

Throughout the film Vicky provided a running commentary on the action, a service which was not appreciated by those around her. When everyone laughed at Lee Marvin's early drunken antics, she screamed hysterically, sprayed popcorn over the row in front of her and shouted 'Give him another drink', twice. She cooed in adolescent fashion whenever someone kissed Jane Fonda, shouted 'I knew he'd do that' at frequent intervals, but was surprisingly subdued during the fighting. Several people objected to her behaviour. Half-way through the film, a small fat man made his way across to Joachim, who was not feeling at all adjusted.

'If she doesn't shut up I'll call the manager,' he said.

Joachim sympathized with the little man but he could not risk a scene more terrifying than the one in which he found himself already.

'If you don't go back to your seat I'll break your neck,' he whispered, without venom. The little man scuttled back to his wife.

No one was allowed to miss the humour of the final scenes. Lee Marvin and his horse sagged heavily against a hotel building. This was more than Vicky could bear.

'Look at that horse. Look at that bloody horse. It's drunk.'

Her voice was hysterical, piercing the cigarette smoke with all the music of a fingernail scraping on a blackboard.

Instead of looking at the horse, people in the cinema turned and looked at Vicky. A young voice from the front told her to shut up. The ice-cream seller signalled to an usherette who left purposefully, presumably in pursuit of the manager. There was a restlessness in the audience which made Joachim afraid.

'Come on, Vicky.' He grabbed her arm, dragging her from her seat.

'What do you think you're doing. Leave go.' She followed him out, oblivious of the violent hatred she had generated.

'It's finished. Let's go home.' It was a weak explanation but it would have to do. In the foyer the manager was waiting for them.

'Could I have a word with you, sir?'

'I'm afraid we're in a hurry.' Joachim hustled Vicky to the door. The manager followed them.

'It's just that we'd be grateful if you did not come here again. Not with her, that is.'

Joachim took Vicky to the car which was now surrounded by small boys. He understood the manager's point of view. Every one of us is chained to a position, with a vested interest, a territory, to defend. The small fat man, out for his weekly treat with his wife, committed to enjoying himself. The manager, protecting his clients.

'We've been minding your car, mister.' One of the small boys approached him, palm upwards.

'No you haven't. Robert Owen has been minding the car.'

'Robertowen!' the boy was offended. 'But he doesn't even live round here.'

Vicky and Joachim got into the car while the group of boys discussed what to do about Robert Owen. Vicky was very quiet. Joachim watched her face soften and grow hurt.

'What did that man say to you?'

'What man?'

'The man at the door. The one with the dicky bow?'

'Nothing.'

She put the car in motion and drove it slowly through the darkening city. Here and there, as they crossed other roads, Joachim caught glimpses of the river, shimmering cool and silent behind black warehouses. Above it the sky burned, dark industrial red.

'Do you like me, Joachim?' Vicky spoke with tenderness.

'Yes.' Joachim's reply was honest. He did like her; he wanted, as far as he could, to protect her from the savagery of British Standard Values.

'You're a nice boy. I'm glad you've come to live with us.' Vicky looked at him as the car stopped. For a moment he was able to see her as she must have been, twenty years before; soft, beautiful and girlish. She caught hold of his head and kissed his cheek.

'Thanks for taking me to the pictures.'

Joachim left her at the bottom of the stairs; she said she had things to do. All evening her phone was busy and clients came and went with great frequency.

Joachim put some bread in front of the mousehole, washed, and went to bed. He listened to the wireless, thinking first about Vicky and her problems and then, later, about Christine Murray. Outside, the pubs were closing and parents were coming out of them to collect their children from the shop doorways where they had been sheltering from the light rain.

Later, when he had turned off the wireless, he heard Vicky going into her kitchen. There was a record turning on her old gramophone. Four neutered voices travelled up the stairs, preaching a very dubious gospel:

> Our day will come
> When we'll have everything.
> Our day will come
> When we'll have everything.

3

The river was the oldest part of the city, having been there from the very beginning. Slow, cool and arrogant, ever independent, it came and went as it pleased; for centuries the swell and dip of its relentless tidal pull had given the city an easy rhythm. In the early days, the city had been content to worship the river, to fill its belly with the teeming life it found in its silken pools, to settle slowly on the fertile shores and stare in wonder at this lazy mother monster which dominated its life. The river had teased the city: every so often it had swollen to devour a small shore farmstead; when the fancy had taken it it had breathed thick fog, enveloping everything for miles around in swirling, noxious damp. The river was a temperamental being and the city, growing tired of its mischievous moods, sought to tame it. Walls, high and thick, solid with the strength of concrete and cast iron, to put an end to the flooding. Industrial refuse, horrible with acid, soap and grime, to exterminate the living things. And sewage to take away the pride. The river, humiliated, slapped furiously against the walls, took the filth and sought to throw it on to the city. But the city was strong now and its walls prevailed. Life in the river was destroyed. The river took the carcasses and showed them to the city, stinking and rotten. The city, having tamed the river, now used it as it pleased: the merchants sent out bigger and dirtier ships, the authorities built monstrous dredgers to tear the heart from the sandbanks and the children, who had once fished and tumbled in the clear water, now threw rubbish from the shore.

All the river could do was to retain its temperament. It is now a gelded monster with a vulgar beauty which it uses, with profound versatility, to bewitch the more sensitive elements in the city. But, every so often, it stinks to high heaven as it remembers the glory of times past.

Quentin Tumble lived alone in a flat which overlooked the river. His living-room had stained-glass windows, a parquet floor and three mahogany castellated arches, which made it the envy of his friends. It was the largest apartment in a big house which stood high in an acre of land in the centre of a private park. Quentin Tumble had never enjoyed living there; he regretted having moved in. He had done so to please his wife, who had been very impressed with the view from the window and with the notice at the end of the road which warned that the area was barred to the general public and their dogs. He found the living-room very uncomfortable. It had the atmosphere of a monastic chapter-room and was as cold and draughty as a church hall. His wife, seeking to bring out its true character, had filled it with solid, unyielding Victorian furniture which, at the time, was very fashionable and the envy of her friends. Most of all he disliked the pale stench of decaying sewage which rose from the river to fill his bedroom before he awoke. As soon as he had a free moment he was going to move out.

Quentin Tumble was thirty-seven, slightly bearded and discontent. He was one of that small army of post-war graduates from the London School of Economics currently taking over the new positions of power and influence in British sociology. He was described by those who thought they knew him well as eccentric, an anarchist, a rebel, none of which descriptions suited him. He was not a rebel. It was true that he paid no heed to the conventions of dress and manners but this was not because he sought to challenge these conventions. Like many sociologists he perceived social facts only in the abstract: as mathematical correlations which could be established logically and recorded in articles of pseudo-scholarship in the *British Journal of Sociology*. These social facts need never become part of his life. There are some sociologists who can recognize statistical poverty but not a poor family. Quentin Tumble was rather like that.

He lived alone because his wife had left him. He was not sorry to see her go; she had offended him mortally. Indeed, it was not until she had gone that he was able to appreciate how claustrophobic his life with her had been.

He met her at a summer school in Leicester, where he had read a paper on 'Differing Courtship Patterns in Three North European Towns'. She was then an assistant lecturer at the University of Essex, where she took eighteen-year-old boys and girls on futile journeys along the pleasure-laden paths of Anglo-Saxon grammar. The summer she met Tumble she was dabbling in sociology: everyone, apparently, was doing it that year. Tumble, of course, was the most colourful speaker at the session; courtship patterns were things he knew a great deal about . . . His lecture was joy-making, captivating the heart of Evelyn Beam, who listened, blinded by the dazzle of his purple shirt, trembling at the vision of the historical novels she could bleed from a husband with so much information.

That evening she visited his room, pronounced herself enthralled by his lecture, sat on his knee, seduced him, and ran from the room to announce to the academics in the bar that they were engaged to be married at the end of the week. Tumble was visited by his friends, who thought they had known him well and who confessed that he had surprised them once more with the speed at which he conducted his affairs. Tumble, ignorant of the engagement, thought they were talking about the seduction and was, in consequence, rather embarrassed. Evelyn Beam returned to hug him in full view of his friends who congratulated him and left. Evelyn Beam was pretty and not without guile so that Quentin was left, at the end of the evening, with the clear memory of having been responsible for everything. They were married, as foretold, at the end of the week, just before the summer school finished. The British school of sociology trembled again at Tumble's eccentric behaviour. His reputation was built upon a series of such non-events.

Evelyn Tumble left the University of Essex to take up an appointment as a lecturer at her husband's university. In the four years she was there she made sure that he lost nothing of his reputation. She bought his suits for him, had his shirts hand-made by her dressmaker and filled his house every evening with untalented and vulgar poets. Tumble accepted these invasions as he had accepted Evelyn: uncomfortably convinced that he was responsible for the whole scene. Evelyn talked to him about courtship patterns and he told her everything he knew, tracing the historical developments of the art of wooing, indicating the function of a particular kind of courtship in a particular form of social system, giving her a complete picture of all such habits known from the earliest societies. Evelyn, for her part, gave him nothing. She took his information and turned it into three historical novels, which were received with acclaim by the anonymous critic of the *Times Literary Supplement*. She was applauded for her courage – before her, no one had dared write a detailed historical romance about Stone-Age Britain – and for her scholarship in knowing so much about courtship patterns.

She persuaded her husband to sell his house and to move into the flat overlooking the river. The sale made them rich and it was not long before Evelyn found it necessary to make regular trips to London to visit fashionable literati. Quentin Tumble, meanwhile, became motivated to seek immortality in the procreation of children and, accordingly, got his wife with child. Evelyn, pleased at first, soon tired of the idea and was persuaded by one of their London friends to spend some of her surplus cash on a fashionable abortionist. She returned to Tumble, told him the news, and was promptly pitched out of the flat.

Tumble enjoyed kicking his wife through the door. It was

the first moment of real passion he had known since he married her. When she wrote to ask for a divorce he went willingly to a talented Mrs Oak to provide the legal profession with evidence sufficient to the purpose. The divorce came through, Tumble paid his bills and visited Mrs Oak again, delighted to be free.

In London Evelyn flourished. The world of television drama provided her with the perfect market for her plagiarisms. An anthropological study of Cargo Cults in the South Pacific and a Home Office report on events leading to the closure of an approved school were both transformed into television plays. The Sunday critics admitted that they were humiliated by such versatility. Her third project was frustrated. Having spent five weeks trying to turn *When Prophecy Fails* into yet another play, she was furious when she discovered that another woman had just turned it into a novel. She was not pleased when the critics praised the novel for its sociological merit. Had she been free to do so, she should have liked to be able to expose the fact that the novel had been stolen.

Tumble lived happily enough after the divorce, in spite of the discomfort of the flat and the smell from the river. He was offered chairs at two of the new middle-class universities and his name was now being mentioned in connection with the new chair at Cambridge, a gossip which was flattering but misguided. Two American universities, conveniently ignoring his youthful activities in the Communist Party, had sent out feelers. His career, it seemed, had never been in such health. He was England's most fashionable sociologist.

It is difficult to explain, therefore, how Tumble, in living so happily, was, at the same time, so discontent. It may have had something to do with his colleagues in the Department of Sociology and Social Administration, who annoyed him with their continual chatter of political intrigue. Or it may have had something to do with the mail he was receiving. His fame

as a sociologist had brought in its wake a special kind of responsibility. Professors from all over the country had decided
to use him as a central employment exchange, sending him
long letters about new posts they were creating in their departments, and seeking his advice as to the suitability of this
applicant or that one. But neither of these phenomena were
enough to explain his present frame of mind. The most likely
cause was the new research project he had been asked to supervise.

His professor, Warble, had returned from a Christmas lunch
with the director of one of the new Business schools, fired with
enthusiasm for industrial research. Industrial sociology was in;
every university was doing it; his department wasn't; it must
start at once. Quentin Tumble, Senior Research Lecturer, was
summoned to the foot of the chair one morning and instructed
to set something in motion in the management line. Money
was found, a vacancy for a research assistant created and filled,
a date for publication settled with the University Press. Warble,
or Serendipity Warble as he was called by his staff in view of his
amazing knack of discovering things by accident, had his eye
on a life peerage; the sooner the project was completed and
the country told, the better. His wife, too, was making her
usual parasitic contribution. Two months ago, she had asked
Tumble if she might add two or three questions to his survey
to save her the expense of a questionnaire of her own. Tumble's
questionnaire was concerned with life on the shop floor; she
was preparing a thesis for an M.A. on the causes of Juvenile
Delinquency. It was his duty to merge the two projects and to
collect information which was useful to both.

Tumble was not at all interested in industrial research. He felt
he had still too much to discover about courtship patterns. He
set off for the project meeting feeling rather persecuted.

Joachim, having fed his mouse and shaved his chin, was on

his way out of the house when he was stopped by a little man
at the front door. He wore large spectacles.

'I'm from the Children's Department,' he revealed, with
some feeling of power.

'Really. Well I don't think we want any this morning, thank
you.' Joachim was in good humour: the sun was out, the air
clear, his shirt clean, and he was off to the project meeting. He
felt that the day was full of promise.

'No. You don't understand.' The man stamped his foot impatiently. 'I have reason to believe that there is an illegal nursery in this house and I have come to investigate it.'

'Goodness me.' Joachim looked very concerned. 'An illegal
nursery?'

'Yes. In order to set up a nursery or baby-sitting service it is
necessary to obtain first a licence from the appropriate authority.
I have reason to believe that such a nursery has been arranged in
this house and no licence has ever been issued to anyone here.'
He opened his briefcase and removed a document from it with
all the speed and grace of an insurance salesman. 'I understand
that the nursery is supervised, if one could use that word in
reference to an unqualified person, by a Mrs Prosper.'

You are an obnoxious little man. Joachim looked at him as he
stood on the doorstep, brandishing his document as if it were
Excalibur and he a tried and tested Arthur.

'I've never heard of Mrs Prosper. You must have come to
the wrong house.'

'I've checked with the G.P.O. Mrs Prosper was here yesterday. She received two letters.'

There was no answer to this bureaucratic efficiency. The man
had 'Official' stamped all over him. Checked with the G.P.O.
had he? Was he sure it wasn't the Post Office. Such an untidy
phrase, Post Office, vulgar vernacular. G.P.O. was much
more impressive; it had all the weight and power of a rubber
stamp.

'Piss off,' said Joachim, with no more ado. 'There's no Mrs Prosper here.'

'There is no need to take that attitude,' the little man pouted. 'I must tell you that if you do not let me in I shall return with a constable.'

There he was again. There is no such thing as a policeman. Only constables, sergeants and chief inspectors, neatly arranged in rigid hierarchical order. Joachim bent down and looked hard into the man's spectacles. 'Piss off.'

The official from the Children's Department stepped back in distress. He was only doing his job after all. There was no need for such vulgarity. Someone had to do it. It was not very pleasant at the best of times, but it was good work and it had to be done. The Home Office was encouraging Children's Departments to expand. Hit the problem before the problem hits you was the new concept in child care. Some people did not even know there was a problem. Wait until he was made a Child Care Officer and given some authority. This sort of scene would not, could not, happen then.

'I shall be back with a constable and I must warn you that your behaviour will be reported.'

Joachim took an aggressive step towards him and he scurried off down the street. As he passed in front of the wilderness an egg was thrown at him from an upstairs window. It missed his head but it landed on the pavement beside his trousers, covering them in yellow slime.

'What's all this noise about?' Vicky had come out of her bedroom wearing acres of dressing-gown. She approached Joachim who was still at the front door in the sunshine.

'Some idiot from the Children's Department. Said there was a Mrs Prosper here running an illegal nursery.'

'You didn't let him in, did you?'

'No. He says he is bringing a policeman.'

'He says that every time but he never does.'

'Why, how often does he come?'

'Every month. He's after Bonnie, downstairs. We never let him in or he'll have her in court.'

'Bonnie?'

'Bonnie Prosper. She looks after people's kids when they go to work. Haven't you heard them screaming the bloody place down in the morning?'

'So there is an illegal nursery. Where are they now then? I can't hear any noise.'

'She always knows when he is coming round so she takes them to her sister's.'

'How does she know?'

'The postman tells her. The man always comes round the day after he asks the postman whether she still lives here and whether she receives letters.'

'That's very clever.'

'No it isn't. It's common sense. Do you want a cup of tea?'

'No thanks. I have to go to work.'

'Please yourself.'

Joachim left the house, his equanimity restored by the news about the postman. On his way into the department he met Christine Murray, who was going in for her first lecture in Criminology. She looked, pointedly, at his cigarette before returning his smile and his greeting.

'Good morning.'

'Good morning.'

She allowed him to hold the door open while she went in but she did not stop to talk to him. Joachim watched her patter off in the direction of the students' cloakrooms. She did look pretty this morning. With no make-up and that innocent mandarin sweater she could have come straight from a convent sixth form. Joachim found such purity very seductive. Having endured a rigid Catholic upbringing, he was very impressed with virginity, but, since he considered himself a liberal, as opposed to an orthodox believer, he did not insist on actual virginity; merely the semblance of it. Christine Murray, being young, firm and clean, caused him some tremulous palpitations as she tripped busily across the floor.

She was not thinking about Joachim. Pressed for an opinion she might have confessed that she found him pleasant, polite and handsome but she would have had to admit that his habit of smoking cigarettes did not meet with her approval. At the moment, however, she had other things to occupy her mind. Her lectures so far had been baffling. They had been full of very long words, had been delivered at high speed in dark rooms where she could not see what notes she was writing, and had been meaningless. To add to her advance reading list she had taken down the titles of twenty-three studies, all, she was assured, indispensable reading matter for the examinations. Criminology might be less obscure, though she hoped there would not be too much emphasis on crime statistics – her maths was very weak.

She was meeting Hazel for lunch. Hazel lived in the room next to hers and she was very maladjusted. She smoked very heavily, without ever eating a proper meal so that she was bound to die of lung cancer pretty soon, unless she changed her ways. They had been out to the pictures recently and she had cried all the way through the film, which was very surprising because 'Cat Ballou' was supposed to be funny. Hazel had not been able to explain why she had cried.

'I don't know,' she had said, 'I don't know what the hell I'm doing here.'

She was a very sensitive girl, Hazel. Wherever she went she always made people look at her. Not because she was pretty – she was very thin and deathly pale – but because of the way she behaved. Her eyes were never focused properly; whenever she looked at you she seemed to look through you, right into your soul. It was quite disturbing; she should really wear glasses.

She had to wear them for reading so her eyes must have something wrong with them. It was difficult to imagine how she
could see anything at all through the smoke-screen she lived in.
Daddy said that girls who smoke cigarettes should smoke them
well or not at all. What would he say if he were to see Hazel
Nutt?

Christine took her seat in the lecture hall, which was already
quite full. The other students of the Child Care course were
much older than she was, well two or three years older anyway, and some of them had been working in local authority
welfare departments before coming up to the university. She
took out her note-pad, placed it on the little rail which separated
her row from the row in front, and waited, ball-point poised, for
the lecturer to begin. He was a young man, prematurely bald.

'Criminology,' he began, impressively, 'is the study of those
forms of behaviour which can loosely be called criminal.'

Joachim's fellow research assistants were not in the room they
all shared. Their desks were empty and the room draughty and
cold. Presumably they had all gone down to the common room
for morning coffee. Joachim was not sorry to find the room
empty. Two of the inhabitants were beginning to irritate him,
the one with his over-familiarity, the other with his patholo-
gical phases of withdrawal.

The over-familiar member was Nick Hill, a sophisticate from
Aberystwyth, who handled minor statistical problems in the
department. He assisted the lecturer in statistics who was too
busy preparing to be a sub-dean to bother himself with research. Nick Hill had a blackboard behind his desk, an electric
calculating machine, twelve books of logarithms and a volume
of random numbers. He had recently ordered a typewriter, a
card index system and three boxes of coloured chalks. Of the
four research assistants Nick Hill was the only man who could
not survive in a non-technological situation. Even the words he
used were only ten years old. He collected them at random from

abstruse textbooks in sociology, psychology and their attendant disciplines, and from the fringe vocabulary of the local beat population. His conversation, tinged with chauvinism, expressed in this curious mixture of scientific jargon and psychodelic monosyllables, and accompanied by frequent pats on the cheek and the use of abbreviated Christian names, rendered Nick Hill nauseous to most of the people he considered his close friends. He called Joachim Joke, Jock, or Kim, as the fancy took him.

The other irritant in the room was a wispy thirty-year-old from the United States, who was researching into grass roots political movements in the north of England. He had suffered a great deal at the hands of the English Bolshies at the university, whom he had reported to the local American consul. Born in the American Mid-West, he had grown up in the company of farmers, from whom he had learned to love all things American. The same state which gave Joseph McCarthy to the United States sent our friend on a scholarship to England to see what he could do. What he had done was to go red-hunting in the university and, boy, had he found some reds. There was a Communist Society, a Labour Society, Socialist Society, a New Left Group, all of them out in the open with the declared aim of driving a large wedge between Britain and America. What work there was for him here. He was made welcome at the meetings held by these societies and thrown out as soon as he opened his mouth to speak. Because he suffered so much and because he sat at his desk in silent distress he was called Pentup Emotion. Joachim did know his real name. Nick Hill called him Pent.

The other inhabitant of the room came in through the door just as Joachim sat down at his desk. His name was Gerry.

'Morning, Joachim,' he nodded as he sat down at his desk and put his feet on an upturned waste paper basket. 'Very good of you to turn up.'

Since Quentin Tumble had told Joachim that he would not be needed until the project meeting, his visits to the department had been short and in the afternoon. Gerry's boss required him to be at his desk at nine-fifteen every morning. He never gave Gerry anything to do; he just wanted him to be available in case he was needed. Gerry filled in his time at the department with free-lance journalism and short-story composition. He had the best collection of rejection slips Joachim had ever seen.

'Written any novels this morning?' he said, by way of riposte.

'No.' Gerry kept his feet on the waste paper basket and continued to stare at Joachim, his hands behind his head.

'Where are the other two?' Joachim asked, making conversation.

'Fighting over immigration in the common room. What time does your meeting start?'

'In about five minutes.'

'It should be fun. Tumble has never done any industrial research before.'

'I know. Are you coming?'

'No. I haven't been invited. I should watch Serendipity's wife if I were you. She eats research assistants.'

Joachim liked Gerry. He was not wrapped up in the great game of self-projection which most people working in universities find so time-consuming. Gerry was a healthy young man with a vigorous dislike of the pretentious. He was not seduced by the tactics of the strategic neurotics and he treated both Nick Hill and Pentup Emotion with aggressive scorn. 'You'd better go if you don't want to be late. Serendipity spanks little boys who don't turn up on time,' he said to Joachim who was looking out of the window.

'You're right. Good luck with your poems.' Joachim got out of the room just in time to avoid the waste paper basket which hit the wall behind his head.

The project meeting was due to start at eleven-thirty in the large conference-room on the first floor. When Joachim arrived he found Nick Hill already in attendance. He was smoking a small pipe.

'Hi, Kim, park it.' He waved Joachim to a seat. There were several chairs around a large conference-table. Nick Hill was sitting at one end, his papers and books open in front of him. He did not seem to mind where Joachim sat; when he was king he was a very liberal monarch.

'I didn't know you were coming,' Joachim said to him, implying that if he had known he might have stayed away.

'Statistical analysis, man. You can't run a research project without it.'

'I see.' Joachim did not wish to make the matter controversial. Nick Hill had the skill to turn even the simplest argument into a happening. He sat down at the end of the table farthest from Nick Hill and waited for the others to arrive.

Quentin Tumble was the next through the door. He had a large brown envelope under his arm. Coming through the door he smiled at Joachim and then, with less enthusiasm, at Nick Hill.

'Morning, Ryan. Nice to see you. I hope you are full of ideas this morning. This is something of a new venture you know.'

'Good morning. Perhaps I might have more ideas when we work out what we intend to do. At the moment I am rather confused.'

'Morning, Hill,' Tumble said to Nick. 'I don't think we shall need you at this stage.'

'Agreed, Quent, but Serendipity sent me the royal telegram.'

'He told you to come?'

'As a shepherd calls his dog, Quent.'

'I'd be grateful if you did not call me Quent. I prefer Quentin, or even Tumble.'

At this moment Professor Warble and his wife came into

the room. He was of medium height, plump, bespectacled, with grey hair and two chins. His wife was much taller, thinner and aggressive. They reminded Joachim of a page in his childhood nursery-rhyme book: Mother Hubbard and Humpty Dumpty had looked at each other across the margins.

Warble introduced Joachim to his wife, who extended a lean hand which Joachim snatched from the clouds and waved up and down. Warble then took his seat at the end of the table, gesturing to his wife to sit at his left hand. Joachim and Tumble sat opposite Mrs Warble, while Nick Hill remained where he was, miles away at the other end of the table.

'I asked Hill to look in, Tumble. The business schools seem very interested in mathematics.'

'I expect we shall be able to fit him in.' Tumble, like most people, disliked Nick Hill. Quent indeed. The man hadn't been in the department twelve months.

'Good,' Warble continued. 'Shall we start?'

Tumble nodded, Mrs Warble smiled, Nick Hill raised a permissive hand at the far end of the table. Warble cleared his throat.

'We want something which is useful to industry. None of this abstruse theoretic stuff. There are too many Parsonian grand schemes afoot nowadays. No use to anyone: Let's have something we can get our teeth into, something we can turn into a basis for social action. Find a problem and solve it. Action centred research. Right?'

Tumble waited while the professor made his speech. This happened at every project meeting. The troops were gathered and their morale raised. The professor had lost contact with sociological research as soon as he had taken up his present appointment. Consequently, anything he said about it was usually a load of cods. Newcomers, like Ryan here, were always scandalized, but they learned very quickly that the tactic to employ was to listen, to agree, and then to go away and do what was appropriate, independently of anything that had been said or decided at the project meeting. Project meetings were thus seen as a complete waste of time. They were held merely to keep the professor convinced that he was still making a contribution to the Body of Knowledge that was sociology. Any minute now he would get to his lack of moral fibre homily.

'My wife and I were discussing the negative contributions that industry has made and may still be making to our society. It seems to me that there may be something in the hypothesis that the quality of our environment has been much reduced by the industrial revolution, and that much of the behaviour which is called criminal may well be nothing more than an unconscious attempt on the part of the underprivileged to redress the balance. My wife, as you know, has been researching into the wider causes of juvenile crime – a field in which more rubbish has been written than in any other branch of sociology – and she is convinced that a major condition of pre-pubic criminality is the poverty of the environment of the working classes.'

She has been at the Sunday papers again, Tumble mused uncharitably. Warble was being very clever: problem-centred research in industry and juvenile delinquency explained in the same project. They would make him Queen for that.

'My own view is that living in an industrial society is much more difficult than living in a primitive one. There is no such thing as mental illness in post primitive societies.'

'Only because they've never heard of it,' Joachim muttered, horrified.

'Did you say something, Ryan?' Warble asked, genially.

'No. I was thinking out loud.'

'Well, come on, man. Speak out. That is what we are here for. How can you contribute anything if you never open your mouth to let the words out?' He looked at his wife after he had said this. She smiled at him. This was her husband at work:

witty, in command, drawing the best from the young men around him. This was a born leader.

'It was not a very good idea.' Joachim was rather embarrassed.

'Well if you get a good one come out with it and earn your pay. To continue, it seems to me that industrial society brings with it its own kind of problems and that many of the breakdowns in behaviour, criminal or mental, can be seen in terms of the failure of the mentally ill and the criminal to adjust in the appropriate ways. I thought we might look at this area. No one seems to have covered it adequately before.'

Brilliant, thought Tumble. Mental illness, Juvenile Delinquency, Crime, The Problems of Living in an Industrial Society, all explained in the same project. Short of an enlightening visit from an ambassador of the Great Sociologist in the sky, there was no possible way of tackling this one. Even so, Revelation was not accepted by the British Sociological Association as a valid method of explanation.

'I agree that such a venture is worthwhile and, if achieved, would set British sociology on fifteen years. Unfortunately, I'm afraid I was not prepared for an investigation on so grand a scale. Perhaps, if Mrs Warble could let me have her ideas on a piece of paper sometime this week, then I could design a bigger project than the one I had in mind.'

Tumble had used this technique before. Mrs Warble hated writing anything down. Her 'theories' generally emerged from the mouth of her husband and were nearly always quoted as parts of conversations which had taken place the previous evening. The quickest way to cut the professor down to size was to get at him through his wife.

'*I* am really very busy this week. I would prefer to add two or three questions to the questionnaire.'

'Are we using a questionnaire then?' Tumble looked at the professor. With some luck he might be able to turn the

F

whole project into an investigation of industrial courtship patterns.

'Oh yes. I think we should. What do you think, Ryan, or you, Hill?' The professor prided himself on his ability to widen discussions.

'Once we have decided what information we want and where we are likely to find it, then I think a questionnaire might be appropriate. But at the moment I am still rather confused.' Joachim tried hard to be diplomatic in what he was sure was an insane situation. His comment circled the room like a donkey with three legs.

'Thank you, Ryan. Hill?'

'A pilot run to establish associations, prof. Set up a group of hypotheses; play them up on an interviewing schedule decorated with probes. Systematic sampling, regression coefficients. Round up with tactical participant observation.'

'Thank you, Hill. That seems to wrap it up, Tumble.'

'I think it does.' Tumble examined Nick Hill as a nun would examine a prostitute, with a mixture of disgust and fear.

'Well, my wife and I have a lunch date with the Vice-Chancellor. We can't keep him waiting. I'll leave you to work out the details, Tumble, and perhaps we may have a progress meeting in about four months' time. My wife will let you have her questions as soon as she can.'

Professor and Mrs Warble left the room together. They were hardly out of the door when Nick Hill burst out laughing. Tumble ignored him and addressed a bewildered Joachim.

'I should have warned you about the project meeting, Ryan. I'm afraid that you and I will have to work out this project by ourselves. If we have to include Mrs Warble's questions then we might as well look at several aspects of life and behaviour in the industrial situation. Industry is not the best place to do research of this kind but we are limited to it in this project. I was thinking of something along the lines of a comparative investigation. If we were to take three groups or categories, say, for example, personnel managers, manual workers and scientists and compared their behaviour in two or three areas we might be able to manage something with the money we have. I was thinking of looking at their sub-cultures, in the work situation and outside it, to find out if they differ in significant ways from others who live in the same sub-culture but who work at different kinds of jobs. We would also compare the categories to see if there were significant differences in behaviour between them. I think sexual behaviour should be our first level of inquiry because, as you probably know . . . '

In a small Chinese restaurant near the university lunch was being served at cheap rates to businessmen and students.

'Hazel, must you smoke while I am eating? Why don't you have some lunch? It's good.'

'Christ. I don't know. I can't eat.'

'Please don't swear.'

4

Joachim was shaving in preparation for his first evening out with Christine Murray. It had taken him three weeks to get round to it but then had had no opportunity to set things in motion. Short of lying in wait for the girl and accosting her in the street he had had to wait for an opportune moment. That moment had arrived in the university bookshop that afternoon. Going in to buy another paperback novel he had bumped into her and offered to lend her some of the textbooks she was busy buying. Textbooks are expensive so Christine was delighted to accept his offer. He was taking them round to her room this evening. Then they were going to the pictures.

He left the bathroom with his shaving kit under his arm in a polythene bag. As he went into his flat he was surprised to find a young man on the sofa. He was smoking a cigarette and inexpertly strumming a very pretty mandoline.

'Hello,' said Joachim.

'Hello,' replied the boy, without looking up or ceasing his music.

'I'm Joachim.' Joachim extended a hand, seeking to establish a protocol.

'I know,' replied the boy, ignoring the hand.

'You live here?' Joachim did not give up easily.

'On and off. I came in for some coffee.'

'Sure. Help yourself. I'm in a bit of a hurry otherwise I'd make you some.'

Joachim retired to the sleeping quarters of his flat where he put his polythene bag on the dressing-table and threw his towel on the unmade bed. He took a clean shirt from a drawer and slipped it over his head. He went back into the living-room while he buttoned it up and put on a tie. The boy had not moved; he was still plucking discords from his mandoline.

'What is your name?' asked Joachim.

'You can call me Gordon.' The boy stopped strumming and looked up for the first time. His face was pale and softly feminine, with the melancholic langour of a young Keats. His hair was black and tightly curled, falling carelessly over his forehead in slow symmetrical tumult. But his eyes were his most powerful weapon. His eyes were superb. One was blue, the other brown, and he turned them on Joachim with the wantonness of an adolescent Merlin.

'It's not my real name but it will do for the time being,' he continued.

'Oh,' muttered Joachim, suddenly inarticulate. He returned to his bedroom to recover. He put on his jacket and examined himself rather sadly in the mirror. Until now, he had considered himself handsome.

'You a student, Gordon?' he called out while he combed his hair again.

'Some of the time.' Gordon was strumming his mandoline again. He had paid his tribute to the conventions. Joachim had to raise his voice to be sure of being heard above the minstrelsy.

'What are you studying?'

'Sociology.' The music stopped while Gordon got up to go into the kitchen.

'That's a coincidence.' Joachim came out of the bedroom, having done as much as he could to render his person presentable. Seeing Gordon again he felt he had been wasting his time; there was nothing he could do to approach this casual beauty. 'I work in the Sociology department at the university.'

'I know.' Gordon seemed to know everything. His omniscience and his nonchalant good looks were very irritating.

'How do you know?' Joachim was becoming aggressive.

'I know everything. In any case I have seen you there.' Gordon had picked up a tin of coffee which he tossed cleverly from slender hand to slender hand.

'You know everything?'

'Of course.'

'How fortunate. Why do you need to study then?'

'Because I choose to. Being God, I can choose to do anything I like.'

Gordon picked up his mandoline and walked elegantly to the door, where he stopped and looked back.

'God?' Joachim was horrified at the idea that this youth might be taking the mickey out of him.

'You'll see. Thanks for the coffee. You'll be rewarded a hundredfold.'

Gordon closed the door and went upstairs to his room. Something in Joachim's disbelief brought back the memories of white walls, tough, uniformed orderlies, and long, red, rubber couches. Anodes, cathodes, long strands of wire, red, green and black, sticky rubberlip suckers, white masks, leather chain holding him down. 'NOW.' A switchflick, pain spasms, burning head, legs twitching up and down, on their own, not part of him. Hammer in his head, bang bang at the centre of his eyes; water, blood boiling inside the ears. Snap. Sleep; black watch.

He reached the top of the stairs with the sweat standing out in fine beads beneath his black curls. No time for coffee. He would have to lie down till it passed.

Joachim locked the door of his room before he left. Gordon was either bloody arrogant or he was schizo. He didn't look schizo but if he thought he was God then he must be. Unless, of course, he was God. If the house became a centre for the faith healing of incurables then there might be something in it. Or Joachim could ask the Pope. He was the only person on earth presumed to have a hot-line to the Almighty.

Christine met him at the door with her best smile. She did not go out with boys very often but when she did she knew how to behave. She took him up the stairs, past the Richards' door, which was half-open so that the landlady could keep an eye on who came and went. Her room had been cleaned again, in preparation for the visit so that when Joachim went in he was dazzled by the shining array. The gas fire was hissing merrily beneath the Holman Hunt, the armchair beside it was inviting and comfortable. On the coffee-table lay a neat set of delft, comprising two cups, two saucers, two spoons, two small plates, two knives, a coffee pot, a milk jug, and a small chocolate cake. Joachim removed his overcoat, placed his parcel of text-books on the mantelpiece and sat down in the armchair. This was very nice. Totally bourgeois but comfortable and warm. It was like walking into a dolls' house.

'Would you like some coffee?' Christine asked, with a smile which tickled Joachim's heart. He looked at the coffee-table and could not say no.

'Yes, please. But there was no need to go to all this trouble.'

'It was no trouble. I should have done this for anyone.'

Christine was a very honest girl. It was true that she would have done all this for anyone. If Joachim thought she was treat-ing him as someone special, merely because she had cleaned the flat and had a bath, then he was mistaken. She poured the coffee, handed him a cup, cut him a slice of cake, handed him that and then sat down on the rug in front of him, her legs doubled underneath her body. She was wearing a pale yellow dress made of fine wool, and she had tied her hair with a ribbon of the same colour. The effect was very pleasing.

Joachim thought she looked very pretty and very seductive, sitting there in front of him with the fire throwing shadows on her face. She did not intend to be seductive. The only reason she was sitting on the rug was that there was only one armchair and her visitor was using that. 'I put the books on the mantel-piece.' Joachim looked down at her over his cup.

'Thanks very much. It's very good of you to lend them to me. Textbooks are so expensive and I don't suppose I shall need them after I have finished the course.'

Joachim said nothing for some time. It was so pleasant to sit there in the warm room, an adoring girl at his feet. The October evening closed in quickly, darkening the room, causing the shadows from the flickering gas fire to be thrown on to the wall at the far end of the room. He drank his coffee, finished his cake, put down the cup, saucer and plate and reached into his jacket pocket for his cigarettes. With some luck, they might be able to spend the entire evening here. He noticed that she had a record-player tucked away in a corner and, unless she actually wanted to go out and brave the cold night, they could have a very pleasant evening in her room. She did not look like a sex-kitten and he had no intention of seducing her, but one could never tell. Life was full of surprises.

'Would you mind not smoking till we get outside. I don't have any ashtrays.' Christine was smiling at him but she was firm. Joachim came back to earth.

'Sorry,' he mumbled. 'I should really have asked first.' His cigarette was already lit and the smoke from it curled incessantly through the room, testifying to his lack of politeness. Pretty soon there would be a long streak of ash which he would have to deposit somewhere. The only place he could think of was his pocket.

'Shall I get my coat?' asked Christine, now well and truly in charge.

'Yes, do.'

She got up and took the coffee cups and things out to the kitchen. While she was out, Joachim opened a window to throw away his ash. An icy blast rushed into the room, knocking over some postcards which were standing on the mantelpiece and forcing the cigarette ash over Joachim's jacket.

'You are silly.' Christine came back into the room; she was wearing a green mohair coat over her yellow dress. She was laughing at Joachim who was still struggling to close the window. When he finished his face was very red. The evening was not going as he had hoped. He brushed his hands together to remove the dust and stood looking at Christine, very embarrassed. He was not usually so gauche. At his old university he had been considered something of a wit; girls had never been a problem. He had dealt with them as he had dealt with everything else; with a mixture of careful charm and discreet cynicism. None of them had rebuffed him. None of them had disturbed him. None had resembled Christine Murray.

'Would you like to wash your hands?' Christine asked, to keep the evening moving.

She took Joachim to the bathroom and when he came out she was standing there holding his coat. He took it from her and put it on. In the bathroom he had recovered his composure. For the second time that evening he had been made to look foolish. Now he was going to resume control.

'Where would you like to go?' he asked Christine, who was standing leaning against the banister, her legs crossed beneath her coat and dress, her eyes twinkling.

'I thought you were going to take me to the pictures,' she replied, cheekily.

Joachim buttoned up his overcoat very calmly. Of course he had said he would take her to the pictures and he was going to take her to the pictures. What he wanted to know from the little bitch was which of the many pictures she wanted to see.

'Have you seen "Who's Afraid of Virginia Woolf"?' he asked, looking her straight in the eye.

'No.'

'Then we shall go to see that.' He started to walk down the stairs, presuming she would have the sense to follow. She did.

'Have you seen it?' she called out from behind.

'Yes.'

'Do you often go to see the same film twice?'

'Yes.'

This apology for a conversation was interrupted at the bottom of the stairs. Mrs Richards, attracted by the sound of a male voice, had put her eye to the space created by her slightly opened door. Joachim saw her peering through. He had no hesitation in putting out his tongue, an adolescent gesture he would have avoided had he not felt so distraught. Mrs Richards shut the door at once, very hurt. Christine was terribly amused.

'You are rude,' she said, as soon as they were outside the house.

'I know,' Joachim looked heavenwards as if in despair. 'My doctor says it's incurable.'

Christine laughed. The sound of her voice travelled merrily through the quiet suburban night, making Joachim reflect that perhaps things weren't going too badly after all. He clutched hold of her tender hand and dragged her off to the bus-stop, where they caught a bus to town.

Jenny Oak was the city's first prostitute, a status which was recognized by her clients, who rewarded her handsomely for her talents. It had not been easy to achieve such eminence. From the days of her apprenticeship she had had to keep a close watch on herself, and it was only because she had successfully avoided the multitude of quicksands in her path that she was now able to reign queen in a turbulent land. If any of her contemporaries had possessed her instinct for survival then they would not have found themselves in such unwelcome circumstances. Many had fallen early: two or three careless pregnancies had left them incapable of rendering a regular service, so that they were forced either to solicit random, and sometimes violent, customers, or to settle for half-marriages with desperate men who were prepared to take them, their children and their reputations. Some had pressed on, through the dangerous years when, unless the body was cosseted it declined and became less attractive, without looking after themselves properly. These veterans now relied on the younger practitioners to send them men because in this business only the very young and the very talented can command a regular supply of eager clients. Some of her contemporaries had been forced to live in and out of women's prisons, where they were doing nobody any good.

Vicky Ball had never been in prison but she had let herself go to seed during the important years and now she could not have much time left. The way she was going she would be dead within a year. Not because she was ill or anything but because somebody was going to kill her. She should have given up when she was told, instead of trying to carry on with that type of man. The only men who came to her now were idiots and perverts. If she stopped winning at Bingo she would have to get a job and that would be the end of it.

Any girl who has to keep a packet of photographs under her pillow to get her men excited ought to pack it in. It sometimes happened with drunks and nut-cases but, according to Vicky, it was a regular thing with her. Once you started on that line anything could happen. It only needed one religious maniac and you were a bloody mess on the bed.

And Vicky Ball was a year younger than Jenny herself. They had started at the same time, working the American base at Burtonwood just after the war. From the Americans Jenny had taken enough for a deposit on a house in the city and, as soon as the house was purchased, she left Burtonwood far behind. Vicky had stayed too long: rumour had it that she was still there when the last Yank moved out. She followed Jenny to the city where she entertained the worst of the transient seamen, while Jenny and the more astute of the city prostitutes picked up the cream. Vicky married a seaman and that should have been the end of her career but he beat her up and she tried to make a comeback. With her insides in that shape she should have taken a secretarial course or become a lollipop woman. As it was, she carried on and she went into hospital every year to have her womb scraped.

As for Jenny, she had gone on from strength to strength so that she now numbered among her clients a Chief Constable from the next county, a High Court judge, who visited her when the Crown Court was in session, and Quentin Tumble.

She was not surprised by the phone call from Tumble. He wanted to take her out for a meal, which was very nice of him. He was one of those who refused to treat her as a prostitute. He paid her, but he got his kicks by believing that the seductions were his responsibility and were achieved solely because of his expertise. He insisted that their evenings out took the form of conventional courtship. Sometimes they were so conventional they were boring. They usually began with a meal in a discreet restaurant and they always included a walk by the river. In Tumble's flat there would be drinks, strategic lighting, Miles Davis on the tape-recorder, and, when Tumble thought the moment was opportune, they would retire to the bedroom to frolic merrily for half an hour. Of all her customers he was the most gentle.

He was coming to pick her up to take her for a meal. He had telephoned to see if she was free that evening. She was never free; she was very expensive, but she promised to go out with him. She dressed for the occasion, choosing white lingerie and a cool black crêpe dress, with a single strand of pearls. No earrings, light, careful make-up – enough to darken the eyes and soften the texture of her mouth. When he arrived she was ready for him; she could have been a second violinist with the local symphony orchestra, so modest was her presentation.

Tumble led her to his car, opened the door for her, closed it after she had got in. Inside the car he gave her some flowers which he had stolen from his landlady's garden. She sniffed them appreciatively, pronounced them lovely, and kissed him tenderly on his left ear.

'I have reserved a table at Oily Johnny's,' he told her as the car moved out of the drive.

'That sounds very nice.' She lit a cigarette for each of them, surrendering one to Tumble when he had turned the car and it was cruising slowly along the road. He took it from her, placed it carefully between his lips and then he reached down to turn on the car radio.

'I thought you would approve,' he said, without taking his eyes off the road. Vivaldi's 'Four Seasons' floated out into the night, delicately wrapping them in make-believe before it became entangled with the smoke from their cigarettes and vanished out of the window.

'Would you like to go somewhere for a drink first?'

'As you wish.'

'Very well. I think we should wait till we get there. The pubs in town are so crowded at this time.'

Jenny smiled. He would never take her to a pub in town. There might be someone there who would recognize her. Yet they had this charade every time they went out. Let's go out of town, it's much more civilized. The pubs in town are like cattle markets.

Tumble felt strong and confident. This was something he had never known with Evelyn. Now he was masterful, in charge, the decision maker, controlling the evening, setting the pace.

They drove out of the city, out past the tall concrete lamps which stood rigid at the side of the main highway. They passed the parks and the golf course, slowing down to watch a dark whale of an aeroplane rise grumbling into the night from the airport at the side of the river. They cruised through the dark slums beside the industrial estates, enjoyed the brief glimpse of dark countryside before the next town was upon them, until, with three towns passed and the city far behind them, they came upon Oily Johnny's standing alone in a large car park. There was no other building for half a mile; only a small canal and a railway line which the people in the pub could look at if they were bored.

Tumble opened the car to let Jenny climb out. She waited while he locked the door and then she gave him her arm as he led her into the pub. They were greeted by the landlord who showed them to a table by the window and offered to bring them a drink while they looked at the menu. He came back with a small bitter for Tumble and a Pernod for Jenny. He took their order and disappeared, promising to show them to their table in the dining-room when their meal was ready.

The pub was not overpopulated. Opposite them, in the far corner of the room, a corpulent man in a dinner jacket was resting his fat hand on the well-exposed knee of a young girl. In the bar, through the door, they could see three young executives from I.C.I. laughing and clapping each other on the back. They were drinking pints of bitter and sporting shirts from the advertisements in a distant edition of the *Observer* colour supplement.

'You look very smart tonight.' Jenny released the compliment carefully. Tumble was wearing a white roll-neck sweater beneath his hand-made corduroy suit.

'And you look enchanting. I feel like the man in the Bible who has found a rare treasure, brought back from distant shores.' He smiled at her, sincerely.

'I thought that quotation referred to a virtuous woman.'

'Aren't you a virtuous woman then?' Tumble took her hand; it was as if he were teasing a young girl, out on her first date.

'You know I'm not.' Jenny, in spite of her years of experience, felt herself blush. This delighted Tumble more than anything she could have said.

'I'm sure you are. I've told you before that it is the prostitutes of England who are responsible for the stability of thousands of marriages.'

'You should marry again.'

'Never. Once was enough.'

'You should. Just because one apple is rotten it does not mean that you should never eat another one. That's a lot of rubbish about prostitutes and marriage. They are in it for the money.'

'I've heard worse analogies than that from Charles Pretty. I don't want to marry again. I'm happy enough the way I am.'

'You're wrong. You do need to marry again. A young girl, innocent and weak. Someone you can protect.'

'Rubbish,' interrupted Tumble masterfully. He caught a glimpse of Jenny's white petticoat and felt his stomach turn to water.

'It isn't rubbish. You need a wife.'

The landlord came back to show them to their table in the dining-room where they could carry on with the game.

'It was a game. That's what the film was all about. They had been playing games; their whole relationship was a series of games. At the end the games had to stop. All they had left was themselves and the nitty gritties.'

Joachim and Christine had come out of the cinema and were walking down through the city towards the river. Joachim was trying to explain what the film was all about.

'It wasn't a very pleasant film. They were so cruel to each other. How could they have married in the first place?' Christine felt drained: the film had used up most of her emotional puppy fat.

'Presumably because they loved each other. As their relationship developed they grew more dependent on each other. True it wasn't love in the woman's magazine sense but love it was, all the same.'

'It didn't seem much like love to me. Where are we going?' Christine knew that they had passed her bus-stop.

'I thought we might go for a ride on the ferry.' Joachim was reminded again that he should have asked the girl before deciding on such a course of action. She might get seasick or something.

'How will we get back?'

'The ferry will bring us back. It runs till midnight. What did you think the film was about then, if it wasn't about love?'

Christine tucked her hands in her pockets and pouted. She didn't know what the film had been about. It had frightened her very much, she was sure of that.

'I don't know,' she said. 'Perhaps it was an attack on marital infidelity. Perhaps it was an attack on the self-righteousness of American intellectuals.' It was an attack on something, she knew that much.

'You don't think it was about love then?' Joachim was ready to go to town. Of course she didn't think it was about love. Hadn't she said so?

'No. If it was then I don't know much about love.' Christine stopped to look in a shop window and Joachim was left to waste his next sentence on the night air. He stopped too, while she examined the items one by one. She finished and they walked on.

'I don't suppose I know much about love either,' said Joachim, throwing himself at her feet. Generously, she changed the subject.

'Is it like that at the university?'

'Like what?'

'Well, do lecturers sleep with the wives of professors so that they will be promoted?'

'I've never heard of anyone sleeping with the wife of a professor. Wives of professors are usually pretty old and unattractive. It wouldn't be worth the price. But there is quite a lot of sleeping around. According to the cognoscenti in the common room, two of the women in the Sociology department owe their appointments to their performances in bed. Rumour has it that one of them is prepared to sleep around in the interests of research.'

'How?'

'Well, one of the main problems in social research is gaining entry to the social situation you wish to study. Suppose you wanted to study behaviour on the shop floor. Well, in order to get in there in the first place, you would have to get permission from someone in authority in the firm. Firms are not very willing to let sociologists in to look at things because sociologists generally condemn what they find. If your researcher is a woman and she is prepared to sleep with the works manager and get his permission to do research in his factory then the problem of gaining entry is solved.'

'Golly.' Christine was shocked. Lecturers, like clergymen, had always seemed to her to be above suspicion. This information left a nasty taste in the mouth. It was like seeing a nun urinate behind a bush.

'What is more common is morganatic sex.'

'What?'

'Sex between lecturers and students. The university has very strict rules about it but it happens all the time. Last year a girl in our department got a first when everyone thought she was destined for a lower third. Rumour has it that she was sleeping with Charles Pretty.'

'Who told you all this?'

'It's common-room gossip. I can't remember who told me.'

'Sounds like a pack of lies.'

'Never. As scientists, we sociologists only deal in facts, even in our gossip.'

They arrived at the ferry. Joachim bought the tickets and they went on board. The night was very cold but it was not raining so they went on deck. The city stretched in long lines of lights and dark, mysterious shapes all along the shore. The

G

centre of the city was lit up too, so that some of the tall buildings near the dock were caught by light from behind so that
they stood apart, majestic and frightening, in three-dimensional
strength.

Looking down into the river one could see nothing. Black
pools shimmered and slapped against the sides of the ferry,
reflecting some of the lights on the shoreline, but offering the
stranger no glimpse of what was held in the black and murky
depths. The boat vibrated suddenly as the engines fired. Looking down over the rail, they were able to watch the water
churn into a thick foam. The boat pulled out from the landing
stage, someone threw a cigarette packet into the river and they
were off on their short stimulating journey to the other shore.

They did not speak during the two journeys. It would have
been very difficult to do so; once they were out in the middle of
the river the wind got up so that the words were hardly out of
their mouths when they were whisked away to the sea. Christine stood by the rail, her cheeks tingling as the fresh air bit
into them. On the journey back Joachim stood by her and they
leaned, elbow to elbow, on the rail. In the middle of the river,
when no one else was near, he put his arm round her shoulder
and hugged her towards him. She did not come. Her reaction
was to attach herself more firmly to the rail, her body rigid and
her face serious. Joachim removed his arm immediately.

'Are you afraid of me?' he asked her gently, when they were
safely ashore.

'No. It's just that I don't want to get involved.' She looked
up at him, hoping he would understand; she did not want to
explain the whole business again. He may have understood,
but he did not agree with her, so he determined to make his
point.

'Then you do not know much about love,' he explained, not
without arrogance.

'Love is supposed to be total involvement. To say that you do not want to get involved means that you do not want to be loved.'

'Not at all. When I say that I do not want to get involved I mean that I wish to remain free. For the time being, at any rate.'

'That seems to me a very spurious freedom. It's like the Conservative Party's theory of the freedom of the individual. What they really mean is the freedom to exploit. And that may be what you mean too.'

'Not at all. You make me out to be a monster. Do you want me to love you?'

'I want everybody to love me.'

'Then you are very selfish. I don't want everybody to love me.' Christine withdrew her hand from Joachim's and put it back in her pocket.

'On the contrary. It is your attitude which is selfish. Love, both in the giving and the receiving, is totally unselfish. Love is the complete abnegation of self. It is not possession, which is selfish. You choose not to love or be loved. That seems to me very selfish.'

They climbed on to a bus and their conversation stopped. It would have been embarrassing to continue; Joachim may have wanted the world to love him but he had no confidence in the ability of the general public to understand such a sentiment, were he to announce it on a late bus. When they got off, Christine was even more subdued.

'How do you know so much about love?' she asked, with some sarcasm.

'I went to a good Catholic school and I read the works of St John of the Cross. I also listen to the Beatles and go to see films like "Who's Afraid of Virginia Woolf?"'

'I too went to a good Catholic school and I learned what it was like to get involved. There was a girl there who confessed that she was in love with me and proceeded to make my life a misery. She refused to let me speak to any other girl and even when we went home for the holidays she used to invite herself to come and stay with me. I don't want to go through that again.'

There it was, she had had to explain again after all. Perhaps he would climb off his high horse now.

'I'm sorry,' said Joachim, taking her hand again as they approached her flat. 'You should have told me to shut up before I went so far. But I think that what you described was not love. It was the desire to possess.'

She looked up at him, tears of fury stinging into her eyes. Why did he have to persist with his silly argument? Why must he pursue it to the final word! Why would he not understand?

Quickly, before he knew what had happened, she had kissed him on the cheek and run inside.

5

For some weeks Joachim visited the department of Sociology and Social Administration every day. He would arrive in time for morning coffee and he would leave just after tea and biscuits in the afternoon. In the beginning he had hoped that Quentin Tumble would give him something to do, but he never did. The research project was still in preparation; it lay fallow under a pile of papers in Tumble's filing cabinet. Joachim had asked Tumble if he might help in the design of a pilot questionnaire but Tumble had told him not to bother. There was plenty of time to get the research off the ground in the early part of the Christmas vacation. During term Tumble had enough on his plate with his teaching load in the department and the several invitations he had received from student societies in other universities to lecture at their afternoon tea parties. Joachim was given nothing to do. It was suggested that he might 'get some reading done'. That was all.

So Joachim read till he was sick of reading. He visited the works of Durkheim, Weber, Pareto, Marx, Shills, Parsons, Merton and C. Wright Mills. He studied the researches of Chinoy, Blau, Etzioni, Argyris, Lupton and William Foot Whyte. He relaxed from this to the fascinating anthropological output of Malinowski, Gluckman and Margaret Mead. And he exercised his stiffening mental muscles on the stimulating thoughts of Hegel, Rousseau, T. H. Green, A. J. Ayer and Gilbert Ryle.

He suffered from headaches, boredom, and the soul-destroying certainty that he was engaged on a task that was enormously futile. After four weeks he gave up reading for conversation. In the common room he asked others to join him in discussing the books he had just read. In amongst the rattle of tea cups and the tinkle of sycophantic chatter he journeyed from one inane smile to another, looking for answers to his questions. But his curiosity was born to blush unseen; this assembly was a waste land.

Charles Pretty was very impressed with the accuracy of Joachim's philosophical references; others saw that such instant knowledge was dangerous. It could disturb the nice equilibrium of power and influence which reigned in the common room. A man who spoke as Joachim did could find himself promoted very quickly if he was overheard by the right person. That could not be allowed to happen.

One could get away with a reputation for wit in the common room. One could get away with a reputation for eccentricity, or for immorality, or for sharp business practice, for mental illness or for religious mania. One could be a clown, a comedian, a rake, a tycoon, a psychopath or a nun, and one would be welcomed, clasped to the arid bosom of this assembly. But one could not be a scholar, unless one was a bad scholar. To acquire a reputation for scholarship was to invite victimization.

Scholarship, after all, was the business the university was in. It would seem reasonable that scholars could thrive there, that the man who sought fulfilment in books and in purity of thought could expect nothing but support from colleagues who were supposed to have the same values. Not so. The common room was afraid of scholarship. It organized things along different lines. Its leaders, being mediocre, defended their positions through political manœuvre, not through demonstrations of greater talent. The way to a senior lectureship here was not through brilliant teaching or research: it was through flattery, dishonesty, membership of pressure groups and tactical sex. The girl who planned her campaign at the beauty counter defeated the bibliophile every time.

There was, among them, a smart, thirty-two-year-old who was reputed to maintain her position as an inept lecturer in social administration by her willingness to sit on the knee of Professor Padd, whenever he needed her. She was not worried by her reputation. She got what she wanted and what she wanted most was not to have any black students in her seminar groups.

'You're a fascist,' Joachim told her one morning.

'And you're a nasty little boy, made of slugs and snails and puppy dogs' tails.'

Fascist or not, she was on the list for promotion to a senior lectureship this year. She knew what she was doing. There was no room for idealism in the organization of university departments and the sooner that this young man knew it the better off he would be.

Joachim fared no better in his conversations with the other coffee drinkers. The talk was always of last night's television, or of last year's Bond film, or of the latest *faux pas* committed by Flagg or Warble.

'There he sat, compartment absolutely crowded, everybody looking at him, and he didn't notice a thing.'

'Didn't you tell him?'

'Tell him! No fear. What was I supposed to do? Walk up to him and whisper in his ear "Excuse me, Professor Warble, but I had to tell you that your zip is undone and that your shirt is sticking out, in full view of the general public"?'

'Ha, ha.'

'Then every time he saw me afterwards he would think "That's the bastard who made fun of me on the train". No fear, I want a peaceful life.'

'I don't think he would recognize you. He could never tell the difference between Alec and myself. When we were both students he called me into his office one morning, thinking I was Alec and made me fill in this form for a research grant. It was only when I had signed the thing that he could see that he had got the wrong man. He said "Keep this under your hat,

Plunket. I've been watching your progress for some time now. I thought we'd put you in for this scholarship." I didn't say a word. When I left he asked me to send Alec in. That's how I managed to get an M.A. I'd never have got one otherwise.'

'Didn't Alec go down to the L.S.E. in the end?'

'Yes, he was brilliant.'

Faced with conversations like this, Joachim had no choice but to retire to the room he shared with Gerry, Nick Hill and Pentup Emotion. There too he was faced with farce. Nick Hill spent most of his time muttering jargon and writing numbers and symbols on his blackboard. It was the only way he could work, he said, Pentup Emotion was so morose it was deafening.

Pentup's humour was limited to what he called satire. He would awake from his miserable meditations from time to time to hear the last sentences of a conversation, which he would repeat verbatim and then laugh out loud. Thus:

'. . . if you think you can afford it.'

'If you think you can afford it. Ha, ha.'

He was a devout fan of Peter, Paul and Mary. One day Joachim gave him a paperback copy of Stanley Reynolds's *Better Dead than Red* to shut him up. Pentup loved it. He understood it. It kept him quiet for a whole week until he reached the end and wept. Joachim told him to go back to the beginning again; so he did. Joachim said that if the last chapter upset him so much he should rip it out; so he did. Joachim suggested that he write a different ending; so he did, bribing one of the secretaries to type it out for him and sticking it into the back of his paperback. This pleased him so much that he was able to return to being morose with a sense of having achieved something. He thought Peter, Paul and Mary were the last word in satire.

Sometimes Joachim would go down to the students' common room to play table tennis with Gerry or to talk to Christine

Murray. Joachim liked table tennis. He was a better player than Gerry, who was far too cynical to take any game seriously. Playing table tennis with Gerry was an exercise in temperamental adjustment. If he won, he didn't care; if he lost he didn't care. His cynicism guaranteed him victory whatever the outcome of the game.

One morning Nick Hill joined them for a game. He was left-handed and very flash. While Joachim talked to Christine Murray he took Gerry for a fool, sending him the wrong way time after time, taking him in three straight sets with the arrogant certainty of a king with a serving wench. Joachim had no choice but to play him and to beat him. He had to beat him cruelly, tease him, coax him, serve him, and then, when the moment was ripe, savage him, eat him, reduce him to the state of mind consistent with his status as a fallible, finite human being.

Nick Hill won the toss for service. His first three serves were very fast into Joachim's backhand, spinning off the table enough to nullify Joachim's defensive chop. Three love up, Nick Hill tried a slow, short serve which Joachim anticipated. As the ball fell, swerving, over the net, he waited for it to bounce then he took it at its apogee, his hand whipping over the top of it so that it spun hard into the white line and well out of Nick Hill's reach. Nick Hill served the next ball off the table.

Joachim won the first game easily. The second presented him with more problems but he won that too. In the third game Nick Hill grew wild and erratic, sometimes bringing off the most impossible of passing shots, sometimes failing to return even the simplest of serves. Gerry watched with Christine Murray, both of them silenced by the coldness of Joachim's aggression, both of them delighted when Nick Hill was destroyed.

The game was very fast, with both players striving to make

the other look foolish. At one point Nick Hill was smashing furiously at the little ball while Joachim stood back several feet from the table, moving very easily to the white blur, bending sometimes to pick it up from near the floor, having to change direction often as Nick Hill struck the ball at one side of the table and then at the other. Throughout this rally Christine watched Joachim carefully, without recognizing the symptoms of her condition, unable to explain the tremulous murmurs in her virgin soul.

At the end of the game she felt sorry for Nick Hill but it might teach him not to be so clever in future. Gerry was more perceptive and more cynical.

'Joachim, you're a hearty,' he said as the hero came over. Joachim laughed, knowing it was true. Nick Hill was unrepentant.

'You're lithe, man. Like the willows in the wind. Tame that top-spin and you could go places.' He was sweating profusely.

Christine moved away from him, excusing herself to go to lunch with Hazel. She would see Joachim, as usual, for tea on Sunday.

Joachim had taken to visiting Christine for tea on Sunday afternoons, partly to avoid having tea with Vicky and her weekend lover and partly because he enjoyed having tea with Christine in her warm doll's-house room. Hazel Nutt sometimes joined them, Mrs Richards found excuses to pop in from time to time, but for the most part they were left in peace to converse or to pass the time in whatever fashion they found appropriate. They could not make love so they were left with conversation. The words passed between them like boats across an ocean, without bringing them any closer together.

'Did you go to Mass this morning, Joachim?' Christine asked, as she poured out the tea.

Joachim did not answer at once. The vexed religious question was not something he cared to discuss; it could only separate them further. He knocked some cigarette ash into an ashtray he had stolen from the coffee-room.

'No.'

'Are you going this evening?'

'That would be more correct liturgically. It started out as an evening meal.'

'I know it started out as an evening meal. Don't avoid the issue. Are you going this evening?'

'Will you come with me?'

'I can't. I've got work to do. In any case, I went this morning.'

'Then I'm not going.'

Joachim pushed the end of his cigarette against the base of the ashtray. If he didn't go to Mass today it would be Christine's fault. Nice to be able to share out the guilt like Christmas presents. Christine was furious.

'You should be ashamed of yourself. I want no part of your mortal sin.'

'I don't believe in mortal sin.'

'How convenient for you.' Christine snatched his cup from his hand, threw it on to a tray which he picked up and carried, very noisily, into the kitchen. He might think he was being very clever and independent but every time he did not go to Mass on Sunday he injected more cancer into the mystical body of Christ. She went back into her living-room.

'If you don't go to Mass this evening I shall never speak to you again.'

'But that's blackmail.'

'I don't care.'

'Well, in that case, I'd better go to Mass.'

Christine was relieved. She would have been very reluctant to carry out her threat. But she could not remain on friendly terms with a heretic. Who was that saint who said that what the

Devil wanted more than anything was that nobody should be-lieve he existed?

'Are you going to treat me as a lapsed Catholic?'

'Are you a lapsed Catholic?'

'I don't believe in mortal sin.'

'Well how should I treat you?'

'You don't know whether I have lapsed through laziness or through conviction. I don't miss Mass because I prefer to stay in bed; I don't go because it has no meaning for me. My position is moral, not concupiscent.'

'Your position is wrong and you know it. I'll bet you feel guilty.'

'I always feel guilty.'

'That proves you're wrong. If your conscience was clear you would not feel guilty.'

'It proves I feel guilty. I've felt guilty ever since my first con-fession. One must feel guilty if one is a Catholic; that is what Catholicism is all about. All men are sinful, thanks to Adam and Eve. Being sinful, we must commit sin. Committing sin, we must feel guilty. And we must feel guilty not only for the sins we actually commit but for the sins we would have committed had we been presented with the opportunities. Conscience is nothing more than the ability to feel guilty. My conscience is working very well.'

'How clever you are. You know perfectly well that conscience is no such thing. Conscience is an instinct. It makes us able to discriminate between actions which are right and actions which are wrong.'

'And we all possess this instinct?'

'Of course we do.'

'Then why do we need so many rules and regulations?'

'You know why. Because our consciences need guidance. For heaven's sake, Joachim, you went to a Catholic school. You know all about it. You can explain Original Sin, the Redemption, the Mass and all of it just as well as I can. What on earth is the matter with you?'

'I told you; I don't believe in mortal sin. All I got from my Catholic education is a dead God who lies in my bowels like rotten fruit.'

'What a horrible thing to say.'

'It's true.'

'It's fashionable you mean. Everybody is suddenly seeing through the Catholic church. Let's attack everything we've ever believed in.'

'You are being unfair. Some of us have real doubts and these doubts arise from the fact that the church is, frankly, corrupt.'

'The church is made up of men, certainly, and men, being fallible, are prone to make mistakes. But the church is also divine; it is the Mystical Body of Christ and its life is the life of God.'

Christine finished this sentence on a high note. So far the conversation had been conducted without pause. The silence which now prevailed hung in the room along with Joachim's tobacco smoke, bearing claustrophobic witness to the comedy which had preceded it. Joachim recalled that he had said all these things and heard all these things before. Christine lived, still, in the world of traditional Catholicism. Her ideas on religion were those of the catechism, her morality, the undemanding, unquestioning obedience of the first communicant. Her Catholicism was immature. Before it could have any real meaning she must spend forty days fasting in the desert. Before she could live properly she must die. That, after all, was the first beautiful true paradox of Christianity: life after death.

'Before it can be divine the church must first become human. I thought Christ said that. It is plainly not human; it is a bureaucracy, concerned only with its own survival.'

'There you go again, trying to sum everything up in a sentence.'

The room had grown dark, as it sometimes did when they talked through the afternoon. From downstairs they could hear the several chimes of Mrs Richards's polished clocks. There was nothing Joachim could say which Christine would accept without qualification. No doubt her parish priest had preached to her congregation about the dangerous movements of cynicism and intellectual arrogance which were prominent in certain circles of the church. She had probably noted the remarks of Paul Montini when he had opened the first Synod of Bishops. Certain writers and teachers, he had said, were seeking to devalue the church's currency by marrying it with secular philosophies. Tom o' bedlam crying 'Beware the foul fiend'.

From a distance a church bell swung its persistent summons through the night. *Vox Dei.* The perfect monk leaves a word half-written at the sound of the bell, perceiving in its harsh clamour the essence of the mythology on which his life is built. *Arise, my love, my dove, my beautiful one and come.* Was it mythology or was it truth? None could tell; none was allowed to look.

Joachim got up and put on his coat. He had promised Christine that he would go to Mass that evening.

'You are going to Mass then?' Christine smiled, not because she had won a victory but because she was genuinely pleased.

'Yes. I like going to Mass; it's the sermons I can't stand.'

'Well, while you've been such a good boy, I'll let you sleep during the sermon.' Christine kissed him and he left the house, pursuing the bell which was making so much noise.

The church, when he found it, turned out to be a new one. He had to look carefully before he found the door, so modern was the architecture. Inside there were no plaster statues: only Stations of the Cross in wrought iron, and a crucifix and a Madonna in bronze. In the centre of the church the altar stood alone, reminding Joachim of a circus ring and a pagan temple. Around it, the congregation sat and kneeled on furniture of light wood. Everything in the building smelt of the nineteen-sixties. The church, according to a notice in the foyer, was closed at eight-thirty each evening.

Joachim mused on the paradox the building spoke. Suburban England was full of modern Catholic churches; they stood out like cacti on a lawn from the regular rows of houses, gardens and shopping centres. It seemed that the architecture of the church could cope with a changing world while its clergy remained chained in medieval logic. In Liverpool they could build a vast theatre of a cathedral from the contributions of the homeless poor. We need it, they had said, to bear witness. To bear witness to what?

'In the name of the Father and of the Son and of the Holy Ghost.'

'Amen.'

'Let us go up to the altar of God.'

'To God who gives joy to our youth.'

He hasn't given me much joy, but then what chance has He got with all this lot in the way? Joachim shuffled to his feet with the rest of the congregation to watch the beginning of the Mass. The barren ritual unfolded before him like a bad film. Try as he would, he was not able to involve himself in what was going on. He had, perhaps, been dead too long.

The first Sunday of Advent already? It would be Christmas soon. It used to be a good time, Advent. Warm old churches on cold Sunday mornings, the priest in purple vestments and he, an altar boy in a black cassock and a surplice of pure white, moving quickly over the sanctuary, carrying the book from the Epistle to the Gospel, pouring the water over the priest's fingers, holding the plate underneath the ciborium when the people took the body of God into their mouths.

Now Advent, like Lent, had become for him nothing more than a literary technique: a clever remark here and there in secular conversation. Did Christine have to go through all this? She would be perfectly happy if he were to leave her alone. Must he be the instrument of her defloration?

While Joachim was at Mass, Christine popped in to see Hazel Nutt, who had been able to throw light on some of her earlier problems. She found Hazel behind a long black cigarette holder, reading the colour supplement from one of the day's papers.

'Hazel, do you know anything about religion?'

'Christ, no. Aren't there enough problems around without inventing more?'

'Don't you ever go to church?'

'What the hell for, for God's sake? I never have the time.'

'But you never do anything.'

This was too much for Hazel; she put down her colour supplement, lay back and closed her eyes, hurt to the quick.

Joachim came home from Mass without that sense of spiritual fulfilment which the priest had promised during his sermon. Cars cannot run without petrol, he had observed, they must needs pull into a filling station from time to time to receive the energy necessary for them to go on. Catholics are like cars in that respect: they need the energy of the Mass to carry them through their week.

Joachim carried the crude metaphor home with him. It was as irrelevant as a pain in the tooth. Most of the Catholics who were at the Mass would have had their weeks improved if their church could take time off to improve their conditions of work. Sanctifying Grace dished out by the tankful was no substitute for social justice.

He reached the house at the corner of the wilderness. From the window above the vestibule door a murky yellow light penetrated some feet into the cold night air. There were no children and no dogs. Only the quiet shuffling of prostitutes and the steady traffic of slow cars disturbed the scene of death. From a window high up on the other side of the road came a short, clear scream and then laughter; someone was throwing a party in the grave. Joachim shuddered, as he had when he had seen the children devour the brown rat. Quickly, he went up to his room.

After Christine Murray's bed-sitter his own room, cold and lifeless, reminded him of a monk's cell. When he opened the door his mouse was caught unawares. It was hunting something at the far side of the room and as soon as it saw him it scampered across the carpet with all the speed its terror could supply. In spite of all the biscuits and brown bread he had given it, no relationship had been established beyond the norm. Joachim shuddered again as the mouse ran across his shoe and into the mousehole. There was something in the speed of the animal which disturbed him. He took some stale bread from the cupboard and put it in front of the mousehole before filling the kettle for coffee.

He was sitting there, with his overcoat unfastened but unremoved and his hands wrapped round a cup of coffee, when there was a series of knocks on his door, indicating that there was someone outside who wished to come in. He put the cup on the mantelpiece and went to see who it was, hoping that it would not be Gordon, having had his bellyful of religion that day. It was not Gordon but Jenny Oak, which surprised him.

'May I come in? I want to talk to you,' she said, as he opened the door.

'Of course, Mrs Oak. According to the Rent Acts of 1957 and 1965, I as a tenant, am legally obliged to allow you, a landlord, to enter and inspect my residence at any mutually convenient time.' He was not in very good humour and he felt much worse as soon as he had made this remark.

'My, you are in a bad mood this evening,' Jenny Oak teased, as she passed into the living-room.

'I've got toothache,' replied Joachim, thinking that, having got the conversation off to a bad start, he must continue, fatalistically, in the same vein.

'This room is very cold. Why don't you light a fire? There's no shortage of coal.'

'I have only just come in.' Joachim wondered what the woman wanted at this hour. He was not behind with his rent.

'Well, we can't talk if it's freezing cold.' Jenny Oak picked up the poker and started to rake out the embers and ash from the previous fire.

'Don't do that. You'll get your clothes dirty. I'll do it.' Joachim was embarrassed and guilty at the welcome he had accorded Mrs Oak. He could not have her destroy her clothes merely because he was too lazy to light his own fire.

'Thank you, Joachim. That's the first civilized thing you've said since I came in. You light the fire and I'll go and get something for your toothache.'

Jenny Oak put down the poker and went out of the room. Joachim was good with fires – his mother had often told him that he was sure of a boss's job in Hell – and it was not long before he had a neat pile of paper, wood and coal assembled, ready to be lit. As he put the burning match to the paper Jenny Oak came back into the room with a bottle of Spanish Brandy. 'Well done, Joachim. Now take your coat off and wash your hands and then come and take some of this medicine for your toothache.'

Why did she keep calling him Joachim? She had always used his surname before. And what the hell did she want anyway?

'I haven't really got toothache,' he told her, 'that was supposed to be a joke.'

'Have you any glasses?'

'They're in the cupboard in the kitchen. I'll just wash my hands.'

Joachim dropped his overcoat on to his bed and went out to

the bathroom to wash his hands. While he was there, for some unknown reason, he also washed his face, cleaned his teeth and combed his hair. When he went back into his flat the fire had burned up a little. It cast a warm glow over Mrs Oak, who sat on the sofa in front of it, one hand reaching out to the new warmth of the flames, the other holding a tumbler of brandy on her knee. She was wearing brown velvet trousers, the colour of the brandy, and a paler, cashmere sweater.

'Have some brandy,' she said, as Joachim came in. 'It's very good for toothaches and bad tempers.' She handed him a tumbler, which was half full. He took it from her, sat down in his armchair, drank a little, and felt better. It was good brandy this; it sent a quick shaft of lightning through his throat as he swallowed. He looked at Mrs Oak and waited to hear why she had come.

'Have you met Gordon yet?' she asked.

'Of course. I see him every day.'

'Do you think he is ill?'

'He thinks he is God.'

'Yes, I know. I'm worried about him. Not because he might have a fit or anything and ruin the furniture. I met him the other day and he told me he was having a good run. I think they might take him away again.'

Joachim did not understand what she meant by 'a good run'. The rest of her remarks were clear enough: Take him away meant take him back to a mental hospital; they were, presumably, the authorities, who could not be expected to allow anyone claiming to be God to roam free. Traditionally there were two methods of dealing with such people, imprisonment and crucifixion. Gordon could consider himself safe from crucifixion; modern governments found it expedient to avoid the honest forms of savagery in their administration.

'What does he mean by "having a good run"?'

Jenny took some American cigarettes from her handbag,

gave one to Joachim, and lit them both with an expensive cigarette lighter. The cigarette, incongruously long by English standards, rested trembling between her lips for a second while she inhaled the smoke and deliberated on her reply. Joachim took a long pull on his own cigarette, flicking the ash prematurely into the fire.

'I think he meant that he had had no trouble for a long time. When he first came here he was in a terrible state. They'd just let him out of a mental hospital and he was very frightened. Vicky used to find him sitting on the stairs sometimes, sweating and afraid to move. Just after he came he locked himself in his room for three or four days. He wouldn't come out and he wouldn't let anyone else in. In the end he opened the door to let us in. The room was in a terrible mess and there was blood on the walls where he had been hitting it with his hands. We had to keep him in bed and feed him by hand. I wanted to call a doctor but he went berserk when I told him, so we never did. Instead we kept him quiet with sleeping pills until he returned to normal. He doesn't seem to have had many attacks recently.'

'Then why are you worried about him? The last time I saw him he seemed very well provided for. He was going into his room with a pretty girl who was clinging to his every word. That was about three days ago and I think she is still there.'

'Maybe, but he has never had any problems with girls. They follow him all over the place and he takes that for granted. No, the reason I am worried is that I heard this afternoon that the people at the university are thinking of having him put away.'

'Why?'

'It's something to do with an essay he wrote.'

'Who told you?'

'Quentin Tumble.'

So Mrs Oak knew Quentin Tumble. How the world shrank when you really examined it. She must know him very well to be the recipient of confidences about the activities of the power élites in the university. He looked at her more closely. There was no doubt that she was a very attractive woman. Could it be that she and Tumble were having an affair?

'Well, can't Tumble stop them? He has influence in the university. Surely if he tried hard enough he could put them wise.'

Jenny Oak looked at him through a swirling cloud of blue smoke. This young man was not very generous this evening. From what Tumble had said about him she had expected more co-operation and more sympathy.

'He says he is doing everything he can but he is not getting much help from Gordon. He says the trouble is that Gordon keeps annoying everyone. No one really cares whether he believes that he is God or not. What they are concerned about is the inconvenience. If he could keep quiet, or not try to do so many silly things, he wouldn't bring himself to public notice.'

'Silly things?'

'Well, like trying to stop buses in the street by walking out in the road and holding up his hand, or going into hospitals and telling the patients to get up and walk.'

'I thought he was afraid of hospitals.'

'He's afraid of mental hospitals.'

The fire had burned up well by now. Soft flames flew up the chimney, licking at the black soot. Jenny Oak finished her brandy and refilled her tumbler, gesturing to Joachim to do the same. Joachim felt much warmer than he had for some time. Mellowed a little by the brandy, and the fire, and by the obvious difficulty Mrs Oak found in getting to the point, he relaxed. Lying back in his armchair, he smiled across to her.

'What do you want me to do?' he asked.

'I don't really know. If you could look after Gordon. If you could prevent him from bringing himself into public notice. He has already been fined for jay-walking. Luckily he didn't see the summons and I was able to write his letter to the court and pay his fine.'

'I can't be with him all the time and, even if I could, if he wanted to try his hand at a bit of leper-healing I couldn't stop him.'

'He doesn't try to cure anyone any more. He has given up stopping buses too. When he tries something and it doesn't work he gives up and tries something else.'

'Like what?'

'I don't know. That's the problem. If we knew what he was going to try next we could stop him. It could be anything. Suppose he tried to walk on water or fly out of the window. He could kill himself.'

'I can't think of anything I can do. What is this essay you mentioned?'

'Tumble said it was about sociology. Apparently Gordon said that because he was God he could see everything much more clearly than other people. He could look at the universe from outside, while no one else could. There is enough evidence in the essay to put Gordon away for life, according to Tumble.'

'I see. It sounds as if it might have been an interesting essay.'

'Tumble says it's the best essay he has ever seen from a student but that's not the point. The point is, as I said, that there's enough information in that essay to put Gordon away for life.'

'What do you want me to do? Steal the essay?'

'No. I want you to look after Gordon. I want you to keep him out of trouble.'

'The only thing I can do is have a word with him,' he said, 'but whether that will have any effect or not is difficult to say. If the man is so irrational as to believe that he is God then he is not likely to take any notice of me.'

Jenny Oak smiled at him. Her face expressed gratitude, or at least that is what Joachim thought it expressed. But the smile and the warmth continued and then he was not so sure.

'Well, I suppose that will have to do,' sighed Jenny Oak in resignation. 'But I wish we could do something more.'

That sentence was intended by her to finish the conversation about Gordon, but the tactic was not appreciated by Joachim.

'Shall I go up and see him now?' he asked, warm and generous with the brandy and the fire.

'If you like. I don't suppose it could do any harm. I'll wait here till you get back.'

She poured herself some more brandy and made herself comfortable on the couch, tucking her legs underneath her and leaning back. Joachim got up, put his tumbler on the warm mantelpiece, and went out of the door. Was this what she had really come for, or was she feeling lonely for male company? He went upstairs meditating pleasantly on Mrs Oak, who lay on the couch, rich and soft and mellow, eager for his return. He went upstairs with his mind feasting on the abundance of this fantasy but he did not believe it. When he returned Mrs Oak would pick up her handbag and go home which was, he admitted, what he wanted her to do.

At the top of the house he stopped in front of Gordon's garret and knocked quietly. His conversation with Gordon must be conducted delicately and with great care if he was to avoid giving offence. There was no reply. He knocked again and waited, growing more sure that he was going to mess the whole thing up, feeling clumsy and gauche when he knew that he must move with the grace and subtlety of an angel. There was no reply so he opened the door and looked into the room.

The attic room was bare except for a large bed which stood against a sloping wall beneath a large oblique window. There was a chair beside the bed with some clothes on it and a small table, just recognizable in the darkness at the far side of the room. There was a sense of God in the room, a tangible presence of the spiritual. It was not like the candlegrease and incense cosiness of Catholic churches, or like the splendid overstatements of old cathedrals, where the visitor was made aware of the existence of the spiritual by the impossibility of reconciling its absence. If God was not present in those places then He should be, because that was where the authorities had decided to put Him.

In Gordon's attic the sensation of the presence of the spiritual had none of these negative qualities. It may have found its origin in the work of a joss-stick which had burned beneath the window, mixing with the smell of recent marijuana to lift the room and the objects in it entirely from the level of the material plane. Or it may have found its origin in the pale green light which fell through the window on to the bed and the figures which lay on top of it. Or perhaps it was the figures who were responsible for the mystical presence. They lay on top of the bed, naked and asleep, bathed in the light from the green window. They were statue-still with skin transformed by the light to the texture of marble. As Joachim looked at them their sleep was disturbed for a moment and each moved a modest hand to protect the other's nakedness. Then there was peace again, and stillness, and devastating beauty.

Joachim withdrew, as a stranger might withdraw from the Ark of the Covenant, leaving Gordon and his girl to go back to earth, and Mrs Oak.

She was waiting for him on the couch in front of the fire. The room was much warmer now. She stood up as Joachim came in and he saw that she had opened the top three buttons on her cardigan. He saw too that there was very little brandy left in the bottle. She greeted him with a smile that was half alcohol and half lust. He had not been dreaming before: her interest in Gordon, however genuine, had obviously given way to an interest in himself.

'It didn't take you very long.' She lurched towards him as he came into the living-room. Joachim stepped aside to avoid being flattened against the wall.

'He was asleep,' he told her as she sailed past him on her way to the door. Arriving there safely, she turned off the light.

Joachim watched her with water boiling in his stomach. Coming back towards him she opened her cardigan all the way down. The flickering light from the fire caught her in bizarre shadows and silhouettes, throwing grotesque reflections of her swaying body over the walls of the room. She reached Joachim in a final lurch, throwing her arms about his hot neck.

Joachim had no choice but to run his hands up and down her naked back, a duty he found not unpleasant. She, in her turn, removed his jacket, pulled his shirt from his trousers and sent her fingers skimming across his body, summoning to her purpose all the arts and skills of many years' successful awakenings.

Trembling, they travelled awkwardly towards the bed. There Jenny Oak undressed swiftly and lay back, her hands moving spasmodically in feeble impatience. Joachim stood back and looked at her as she throbbed silently on the counterpane. Never had he received such a generous invitation.

He turned away from her modestly as he removed his trousers. His shyness affected her; he could hear her moaning softly behind his back. Naked, he approached her with his eyes closed. Opening them he saw her reaching for him and he was stirred with a quick life which arrived, like a perfect actor, exactly on cue, making the play unfold smoothly and irrevocably.

'Lift up your gates, O ye princes and be ye lifted up, O eternal gates: and the King of Glory shall enter in.' Joachim remarked as he stood over her.

The fire flickered behind them in a short burst of long licking flames. Then he fell. Down, down, he fell in slow tumultuous pain until, at last, he stopped falling, lost in her multiple liquid foldings. The fire, after its burst of energy and light, ran out of flame. The room was suddenly very dark, and it was allowed to remain so till the morning.

6

The night Joachim spent in bed with Jenny Oak left him exhausted. He was animal enough to relish all the sensations her knowledge could induce, and, young enough, fortunately, to sustain the pleasure until she grew as exhausted as himself. Jenny reigned queen through the dark hours, showering him with riches and patronage with a generosity that was almost disinterested. It was not often that she could practise her art purely for the satisfaction such practice could bring. Here was virgin soil, strong and fertile, which she could stimulate or soften or devour, at her own pace and as the spirit moved her. She worked and rested through the night and each time she worked her purpose was fulfilled and each time she rested she found strength to plan and perpetrate the next stage. By morning her work was complete and she was able to lie back, drunk with that sensation of elation which overwhelms the artist when he has excelled himself.

Joachim, the clay, as it were, in which this masterpiece was worked, was forced to think again about the fun and games when he became aware of the consequences it had on his other relationships. He was not one of these modern young men, who can leap into a different bed every night with no more twinges of conscience than those necessary to effect a change of underpants between adventures. His Catholic education had made sure that he could never divorce an act from its consequences and it was these consequences which bothered him. Had he still believed in mortal sin, he should certainly have worried about that but as he had rejected mortal sin as a medieval superstition the only consequences he worried about were mundane and human. He mourned the death of his relationship with Christine Murray. He had felt guilty enough before, when all he had done was to point out to her certain facts of life about the nature of the bureaucratic church. He could not pretend that the bedding of Jenny Oak had nothing to do with Christine Murray. It had changed him and it had, therefore, changed his relationship with Christine. It had taken him farther away from her. To seek to continue the relationship in its previous form would be to deny the truth of what had happened to him. To seek to develop the relationship, in the light of what had happened to him, would be to turn himself into a predator. The bedding of Jenny Oak, pleasant as it may have been, had destroyed, for ever, his innocent affair with Christine Murray. That was a fact of life.

Any convent chaplain would have been delighted to tell Joachim that what he really felt was remorse at having sinned. In rejecting sin and the confessional, where sins are sold for penances, Joachim was punishing himself in his own way. If only Joachim could see that his behaviour gave the lie to his words. He did not believe in sin, he said, and here he was separating himself from Christine Murray because he felt evil. The sense of sin was everywhere: in his feelings of guilt at what he had done; in his unwillingness to bring his defiled person into the innocent presence of Christine Murray; and in his determination to punish himself. Five minutes in the confessional and he could be rid of all these problems; an act of contrition could take him back to where he had left off.

Joachim's uncle was a convent chaplain and Joachim had decided, a long time ago, that, come the revolution, convent chaplains and insurance societies would be the first to go. This was an extreme point of view arrived at under some pressure. Had he taken time off to view the situation more objectively, he would have been forced to admit that convent chaplains, like lions, are safe enough left alone in their natural habitat; they only become dangerous when they are allowed to wander free in human communities which they cannot understand and upon which they must prey, if only to keep themselves alive.

The first indication that his life had been changed by the bedding of Jenny Oak came to Joachim in the reaction of Vicky Ball. She had seen Jenny leave the house and drive away in her car, which had been parked in front of her bedroom window all night. Going to Joachim's room with his mail she had found him in bed, evidence of the night's debauchery to be seen in the lipstick-stained sheets and the pair of stockings which Jenny Oak had left hanging from the mirror on the dressing-table. Vicky threw the mail at Joachim – he was never able to understand how she managed to enter his room through the locked door – and left the room in disgust, muttering unmentionable expletives. Later that morning Joachim was invited to witness the fullness of her anger.

He had to go down for his milk, which she had not brought up with his mail. She heard him coming down the stairs. As he passed her living-room she shouted:

'Some dirty buggers are going to get the sack if they don't start getting up earlier.'

Joachim, who had expected the remark, or something similar, picked up his milk and walked into her living-room.

'Did you say something, Vicky?' he asked innocently.

Vicky did not look at him as he came in. She was sitting on her tumbledown sofa, cuddling a rag doll, stroking its head and pressing it hard against her dry breast. She took a deep breath, as if to imply that her patience was being sorely tried.

'I said that you will lose your job if you don't stop staying in bed all morning.'

'Don't worry, Vicky. I do my work at home.'

First blood to Joachim. You'll never take him with that line of argument, Vicky. He can always use his status. The academic 'we are not as other men' approach. You will have to try something else if you want to beat him down.

'I've run out of coal,' she replied, without ceasing her maternal rituals with the substitute baby.

'Would you like me to get some for you?'

'If you think you can manage to carry it.'

She must get to the point soon. This series of fringe skirmishes was bothering Joachim more than anything she might say about Jenny Oak. In his frustration he faltered.

'Why shouldn't I be able to carry it? I've always carried it up for you before.'

Vicky fixed her eyes on his. Here was her moment. Here was her opportunity to punish him for the fun he had had with Jenny Oak, keeping her awake all night and driving her purple with jealousy. He stood waiting for the blow, as a rabbit, hypnotized by the bright lights of an approaching car, waits to be run over.

'You look very tired. Didn't you sleep last night?'

'On the contrary. I slept very well.' Joachim was relieved that her attack had been so easy to pass off. But she hadn't finished.

'You're a bloody liar. I saw her leave this morning, the cradle-snatching bitch. How much did she charge you?'

Joachim shifted his bottle of milk from one hand to the other, feeling very much the same emotions as he had felt the first time he was reprimanded by his headmaster for smoking in the school lavatories.

'Charge me? What are you talking about?' Jenny Oak could not be a prostitute too. Joachim was very confused.

'So she let you have it for nothing. You are a lucky boy.'

'Vicky, what the hell are you talking about?' It was a foolish question because Joachim knew what she was talking about. He asked it because he was confused and because he had to say something.

'Don't look as though butter wouldn't melt in your mouth. Didn't you know she was on the game? Didn't she tell you what she charges? Ten pounds short time, twenty-five pounds all night, drinks and accessories extra. Where do you think she gets all her bloody money from?'

Joachim sat down to think about all this. He had never sus-
pected Jenny Oak of being anything other than an attractive,
middle-aged, wealthy housewife. He thought of Tumble, of
Tumble's relationship with Jenny Oak, of the many delicious
pleasures she had done to him in the night. She had every right
to be a prostitute and she was probably a very good prostitute
but if he had known that last night he would not have leapt
into bed with her so willingly. He had felt guilty enough about
sleeping with her when he thought she was a housewife. He felt
even worse now that she was a prostitute. And he felt guilty
because he felt worse. He should be able to think of her and
treat her as an individual, as a human being in her own right.
As guilt piled on guilt he sought to rationalize. Why was Vicky
so jealous? Was she jealous of Jenny Oak because Jenny Oak
was a better and more prosperous prostitute? Or was she jealous because she was jealous of any woman who might come
near him? How could she, a prostitute herself, condemn the
harlotry of another? She complained because Jenny Oak had
kept secret from Joachim the source of her wealth while she
herself was guilty of the same deceit.

'She should be ashamed of herself. She can get a man anywhere she wants without bringing her dirty washing here.'

Joachim did not see the significance of the dirty washing,
unless Vicky was referring to the stockings which Jenny Oak
had left on his dressing-table. One thing was clear from the
remark, however; Vicky was envious of the ease with which
their landlady could procure clients. Was her own practice
suffering? At any rate she seemed to have forgotten about the
coal.

'Go and get my coal and we will have a cup of tea.' Vicky,
sure that all her arrows had gone home, was softening. Curiously,
she seemed not to blame Joachim for what had happened.

They drank their tea in front of the fire which Joachim made
with the coal he had brought up from the cellar. There was a

room in the cellar which was inhabited by Bonnie Prosper, the criminal kindergarten boss, whom Joachim had not encountered even though he had been living in the house now for three months. As he filled the coal bucket he could hear the children playing in the room; there was laughter and the sound of one child crying. The sociologist in Joachim stirred at the sight of the locked door and made him determine to go and have a look at the nursery one day before the police moved in.

In front of the fire Vicky told Joachim all she knew about Jenny Oak. Though the extent of her knowledge sometimes gave her away, she conducted the conversation in puritanical terms, condemning not only Jenny Oak but the whole operation of prostitution with a vehemence which would have done credit to a meeting of the Women's Institute. This did not surprise Joachim. He had seen politicians morally condemn politics, clergymen morally condemn organized religion, soldiers condemn war, undertakers mourn. He had known plumbers who hated plumbing, criminals who condemned crime, abortionists with children. It did not seem inconsistent that Vicky, being a prostitute, should despise prostitution. He was growing more disillusioned each day with his own chosen career and he knew it would not be long before he, an academic, would despise academic life.

Vicky continued her onslaught until lunchtime, carefully absolving Joachim of any guilt he might have felt for his part in the proceedings. She invited Joachim to lunch with her but he said he had an appointment elsewhere and she let him leave. He did not go far; having left the house he made straight for a small pub near the university, where he could sit and ponder the information Vicky had just given him.

The pub was one frequented by the local beats, art students, poets and unemployed anarchists. They were not rich clients but there was a great number of them so the landlord, with an opportunism rare in his profession, had allowed the pub to adapt itself to their needs and tastes. It was dirty, sprayed with sawdust and spittoons, into which the customers threw their cigarettes and their memories of wasted opportunities. The beer was invariably stale but it did not displease the hordes of sixteen-year-old girls who came night after night, hungry for kicks and for the sight of the poets. The pub had the atmosphere of a rancid meat pie.

Watching the sediment floating in his beer, Joachim set his mind to sort out the truth from the fiction in the stories Vicky had told him. Apparently the room next to his was not empty, as he had supposed. Instead it was used by two couples on two separate nights each week for extra marital activities. Each couple thought they had a monopoly of the room. They both paid a full week's rent of ten pounds, even though they each used it only for a night. Other rooms in the house were used in similar ways. Sometimes Jenny Oak would bring clients there, sometimes she would lend them to her colleagues, on a commission basis, for parties, orgies, pornographic film shows and psychedelic sex. He and Gordon were there to act as a front for the real purpose of the house. That is why Jenny Oak did not care about their rent – Gordon, apparently, paid no rent at all – what she got from them was so paltry that it did not matter to her. She made more money from a single party than she took from Joachim in a whole term.

How much of this was true and how much of it was the produce of Vicky's jealousy could not be distinguished. He recalled that he had met none of the tenants of the house apart from Vicky and Gordon, but then he had lived in large houses before, when the last thing he had wanted was to grow hearty with the other tenants. He had stayed away from them and he had hoped that they would stay away from him. He had gone about things in much the same way in his present flat, relieved that the only relationships he had formed were those concerning Gordon and Vicky.

I

He drank his beer, filling his stomach with those foreign bodies which had been circling in his glass, before leaving for the Students' Union where he bought a punishing lunch of heavy chips and old fish. Later that afternoon he felt very ill and he spent an hour in bed, his doubts about Jenny Oak still unresolved. But Vicky had conceived of a plan to convince him and later that night, at about two o'clock in the morning to be precise, she put it into practice with fine cunning and a great deal of noise.

Joachim was so ill that he could not bring himself to leave his bed for any length of time. He made himself a cup of coffee each time he awoke but his problems, physical and psychological, seemed to him so labyrinthine and confused that he preferred to sleep through them until he was stronger. There was no comfort in his transistor radio which babbled fatuous protestations of pubescent love mingled in synthetic nursery rhymes every time he turned it on. His paperback novel seemed more than usually epigrammatic and less than usually informed: having passed through his novitiate he was no longer impressed by the opium of the postulants. So he slept, fretfully and uncomfortably, awakening often. At midnight he heard the sounds of a party in the room next to his but when he got up to investigate there was nobody there. Back in bed, it seemed that the party had moved upstairs; there were bumps, jumps and music coming from the ceiling. Defeated, he pulled the blankets over his head and tried to go back to sleep. He had not been asleep long when it happened. Just as the lights in the streets dimmed and the traffic dwindled to its customary silent crawl, Vicky left her living-room to stand at the bottom of the stairs, where she took a deep breath and shouted at the top of her raucous, safe-breaking voice.

'Help! Robbery! Come quickly, I've been robbed. Joachim. Joachim. Help!'

And, to make sure that Joachim did not sleep through her

performance, she ran upstairs, burst through his door, and jumped on his bed. Joachim had been stirred by the screaming, but he had missed the meaning of the words and his first reaction when he woke up and saw the delirious diaphonous creature on his bed was to reach for his rosary beads and to regret every word of criticism he had uttered concerning faith or morals. This visitation could have no foundation in natural law.

'Joachim! Get up. I've been robbed. Come and see. Come on!'

The sound of her voice saved him. That and the lights of a passing car which enabled him to pick out the shape of her starved body underneath the acres of transparent chiffon she wore as a négligée-dressing-gown. He sank back into his bed, very relieved.

'What are you doing? Get up, you bugger. I've been robbed. Come and have a look.'

Joachim got up, picked up his overcoat, put it on over his pyjamas and followed her downstairs. Was this, he thought uncharitably, Vicky's silly way of trying to redress the balance with Jenny Oak? Did she think that, if she got him downstairs in the middle of the night, he might be prevailed upon to stay there, with her?

It was interesting that he could resume his egoism and his misjudgements so soon after being frightened into superstitious practices. Vicky had no intention of dragging him into bed with her. Her plans for this particular evening were much more complicated than that. He did her, as he was accustomed to do most of the people he patronized, a grave injustice.

'There was fifty pounds in a box in that drawer and it's gone.' Vicky pointed dramatically at a sideboard which stood, like a boy with his pants down, at the right side of the fireplace. The drawers had been removed, the cupboards emptied and their contents scattered in an untidy heap in front of it. Above the sideboard was a newly erected picture of the Apparition of Fatima, a clever technique of Vicky's to intensify the impression of the evil done her. It was impossible to look at the naked sideboard without seeing the picture; anyone who could rob a poor woman in full view of Our Lady of Fatima and those three innocent children must be thoroughly evil.

'When did you see it last?' If Joachim was to be of any use to Vicky he must seek to establish certain facts; when the crime took place, who might have done it, that sort of thing.

'It was there this afternoon. I put my Bingo money in it when I came home. There were three packets in it. That was seventy-five pounds, and when I put the other one in it came to a hundred.'

'Well what happened to the other fifty?'

'What other fifty?'

'You said you had lost fifty pounds. If there was a hundred pounds in the box then there must be fifty left.' Joachim felt like a schoolteacher collecting dinner money.

'No. There's nothing left. They took it all, the bastards.'

Vicky was more dramatic than usual. She paced the floor, wrung her hands, swore, sat down, got up, rifled through the heap of clothes and biscuit tins which the sideboard had vomited on to the stained carpet.

'Have you been out since then?' Joachim was pursuing the investigation logically, taking the possibilities in chronological order and eliminating them one by one.

'Since when?' Vicky got up from the heap. 'It's not there.'

'Since you saw it this afternoon?'

'No.'

'Well, have you had any visitors this evening?'

'No.'

'Then it must still be here. If you didn't go out and no one came in then your box couldn't have gone, unless it walked out when you weren't looking.'

Vicky looked at Joachim as if he had insulted her mother. 'You don't believe me, do you? You think I am making it up, don't you? Why should I make it up? I tell you I've been robbed. I'll prove it; I'll ring the police.'

The prospect of being visited by the police when he was alone in his pyjamas and overcoat in the flat of an old and not very attractive prostitute, no more adequately dressed than himself, did not appeal to Joachim.

'Of course I believe you, Vicky. But there's no need to ring the police yet. We might still find it. You go and make a cup of tea and I'll look for it. What does it look like?'

Vicky softened a little at this expression of sympathy. She got up from the sofa, wrapped her chiffon round her body and shivered as she realized that it was the middle of the night in December and there was no fire.

'I told you it's a cash-box, a green one. It was in that left-hand drawer.'

'How big is it?'

'It's a bloody cash-box. It's the same size as a cash-box.' Her face had gone very white and Joachim noticed, for the first time that night, that she looked very old and very haggard. Goosepimples rose and multiplied across her bare arms.

'Go and make some tea, Vicky. And put some clothes on before you freeze to death.'

Vicky went out into the kitchen to put on the kettle. While she was away Joachim completed a thorough search of the room, finding interesting objects in interesting places but failing to discover a green cash-box.

Vicky came back into the room with tea and biscuits on a tray. She was wearing what appeared to Joachim to be an eiderdown but it was, in fact, a quilted housecoat.

'I've just remembered. I did go out at eleven o'clock to get some cigarettes from the machine.'

Joachim knew the machine she meant; it was a good ten

minutes' walk. There were other machines not so far away but they had been broken by children short of toys.

'Then someone could have come in while you were out. Did you leave the door open?'

Vicky stopped pouring the tea and assumed the television pose of someone trying to remember something exactly.

'I closed this door but I left the front door open. Yes, that's what I did. I closed this door but I left the front door open.' She continued pouring the tea.

'The front door is always left open and any fool could break in here.'

'How?'

'I'll show you. It might come in useful if you ever lock yourself out.'

Joachim took Vicky by the hand to the hall, where he closed the door of her flat. She protested when he closed the door, because she wanted to give the impression that she did not believe that he could open it again without a key. But she allowed him to close the door and stood back while he went to the kitchen whence he brought a knife which he inserted in the small space between the door and the joist, at the exact point where the lock made contact with its mate. He pushed the knife in, forced the lock back, and opened the door. The way Joachim did it, the technique was a much quicker and easier method of opening a door than using a key.

'I didn't know you could do that,' Vicky said, very impressed. 'Where did you learn that?'

She knew perfectly well where he had learned it. Such knowledge is part of bed-sit culture and she had been living in rooms much longer than he had.

'Never mind where I learned it. It proves that anyone could have got in here while you were out. That must have been how your money disappeared.'

'I'll phone the police.' Vicky lifted the phone and was through to the police station before Joachim could think of a way of stopping her.

'I've been robbed. Tonight. I went out for some cigarettes and while I was out somebody broke into my flat and took my cash-box. A hundred and fifty pounds.'

Joachim listened while the police sought to make sense of Vicky's emotional outbursts. They would be round here soon. If they were coming then Vicky ought to phone the landlady. They would probably search the house. He thought of Gordon, suddenly. A visit from the police could not be good for Gordon. They were bound to suspect him as soon as they found him. As soon as Vicky put down the phone Joachim told her to ring the landlady while he went to warn Gordon.

He went up the stairs two at a time, so that by the time he reached Gordon's attic he was out of breath. He knocked on the door, as he had done the previous evening, but there was no reply. The door was not locked and it opened as soon as he turned the handle. Gordon was gone. The room was empty, except for the green light and the unmade bed. Joachim turned and ran downstairs, one of his problems solved.

Vicky was talking to Jenny Oak as he came into the room. From what Vicky was saying, it seemed that Jenny Oak was not keen on coming round to the house to sort out the business of the robbery but as soon as Vicky told her that the police were already on their way there was a long silence while Vicky listened to her reaction. Jenny Oak was angry; she was coming round at once. Vicky turned from the phone, rather disgusted.

'She says I shouldn't have called the police. Get the house a bad name, she says. She should worry. The police know all about her. Anyway she's not the one who's been robbed. You didn't hear any noises when you were upstairs, did you?'

'No. Why?'

'No reason. Where did you go anyway?'

'I went to warn Gordon that the police were coming.'

'I could have saved you the trouble. Here, have a ciggy. He's gone to London with his girl-friend.'

'What for?'

'He was running away from some men. That bitch,' Vicky gestured disdainfully in the direction of the telephone, 'rang this afternoon, just after you left. She said some men were coming round for Gordon and would I warn him. Don't know what she thinks I am. I don't mind being the caretaker but I am not everybody's slave.'

'What happened?'

'Well, I told him. He was still in bed, the lazy bugger. Had a girl with him as well. To look at her you'd think butter wouldn't melt in her mouth. Still I put the fear of God into them. Should have seen them run.'

'And did the men come round?'

'Just as I was going out to Bingo. I told them Gordon had gone but they wouldn't believe me. Said I had to let them in, said he was a menace to the community and had to be locked up. Anyway they looked for him and they didn't find him and I was late for Bingo.'

'Did you tell them where he had gone?'

'Don't talk daft. I told them if they came round here again at this time of day I'd pour a bucket of water over the lot of them.'

'Where did they come from?'

'From the university of course. Isn't that where he works. A couple of them had uniforms, like traffic wardens.'

'Porters,' Joachim thought out loud. So Jenny Oak had been right about Gordon. They were after him and they were bound to catch him sooner or later. By the very nature of his illness he was bound to be discovered. Where was he making for in London? Westminster Abbey or Hyde Park Corner?

'What do you need porters for at the university? To carry

your books?' Vicky seemed to have forgotten that she was supposed to be a damsel in distress.

A key turned in the lock of the front door and two pairs of high heels hurried to Vicky's door and into the room; Jenny Oak had arrived with a colleague, a woman who looked more like a prostitute than any woman Joachim had ever seen.

'Go and get dressed, Joachim,' Jenny barked at him as soon as she saw him. How different she was from the previous encounter when she had been so eager not to offend him. She then launched into a conversation with Vicky in which she attempted, simultaneously, to reprimand her for filling the house with policemen and to offer sympathy for the bereavement. It didn't come off.

A knock at the door signified the arrival of the police. Joachim, who felt suddenly irrelevant, went to let them in. As soon as they came into the room it was obvious that they couldn't care less whether Vicky had been robbed or not. A sycophantic sergeant had brought his superior officer to a house of ill repute. They had come along for the ride, that was all. Here was an excuse to have a look at the place without actually raiding it. Good, we'll go and see how the old girls are doing. Give them a bit of a fright and remind them of their social obligations. Make sure that they remember that we could get them any time we wanted.

All this was evident in the sneer of the inspector as he walked into the room and in the interview he conducted with Jenny Oak.

'So there's been a robbery,' he said, contributing nothing, as he came in through the door.

'Yes. I've been robbed. There was over a hundred and fifty pounds in a green cash-box in that drawer in that sideboard and it's disappeared.' Vicky, well wrapped in her eiderdown was unabashed.

'And when did you see it last?' the inspector asked, in routine fashion. He did not look at her. His remark was addressed to the sofa as he took a cool professional police photograph of the room. Swiftly, with brilliant distinction, this scene was being recorded on the black ice of his retina. He patted his hand with his stick a couple of times and each time he did so Jenny Oak flinched.

'The details, Sergeant.' He waved, administratively, at his subordinate and the man was at Vicky's side at once, his notebook out, his pencil sharp, ready to record the details, times, places, people, anything which might throw light on the problem.

'And who are you?' he said to Jenny Oak, knowing full well who she was. There was a photograph of her with no clothes on, in the bottom right-hand drawer of his desk.

'I am Mrs Oak.' She was nervous. 'I own this house. I came as soon as I heard.'

'Jenny Oak?' The policeman raised his stick as if he were about to strike her.

'Yes.'

'*The* Jenny Oak?' He was driving the nails in slowly; that way there was more pain.

'Look, Inspector, whatever else you may know about me this is my house and it is respectable.' Joachim had seen her in many situations but he had never seen her crawl. She was crawling now. Everything Vicky had told him must be true then.

'I'm sure it is.' The inspector's smile broadened as he approached Jenny Oak's companion.

'If she is Jenny Oak,' he paused for effect, 'then you must be Bernadette.' The woman nodded and blushed.

'I've often thought that your name was inappropriate. It conjures up the wrong image. Very unprofessional. I should change it if I were you.'

What a hateful man. Why can't he leave them alone? Perhaps the little bastard gets his kicks this way. Cat and Mouse.

Joachim disliked the inspector more every minute. As the man approached he was aware of a strong urge to seize him by the throat and ram his stick through his ears. But he was standing there in his pyjamas, and the man was a policeman.

'And who are you, Rip Van Winkle?' the inspector joked.

'Surprisingly, no. I am a respectable tenant in Mrs Oak's respectable house, which I would recommend to anyone I know as a perfect place in which to spend one's early, middle, late, and declining years.'

'Your name, lad.' The inspector obviously liked to monopolize all the sarcasm which came into his conversations.

'Joachim Ignatius Ryan, bachelor of arts, doctor of philosophy pending, centurion in the Legion of Mary, retired.'

Joachim caught sight of Jenny Oak gesturing him to give up. This man was a policeman and a firm believer in might is right. Against him no one could win, except a mightier and rightier policeman.

'Do you want to spend the rest of the night in a cell, Ryan?' The police inspector barked, as he had been trained to.

'No.'

'Is there no one else in the house?' The inspector turned, with the speed of light to Jenny Oak, hoping to catch her off her guard.

'No.'

'Search the house, Sergeant.' The sergeant left the room.

With everything very quiet and still the inspector took a long slow walk around the room, eventually pausing at the door.

'You say someone broke in through this door? Easiest thing in the world. I'll show you.'

He took a knife from the table and went out of the room, returning immediately, having opened the door by the method Joachim had demonstrated earlier.

'Any idiot can get in through a lock like that. Padlocks are the answer. You're asking to be burgled with a lock like that.'

The sergeant returned, expressionless and obedient. He stood in the doorway, waiting to be spoken to before he himself would speak.

'Did you find anything, Sergeant?'

'There were three men in bed with a woman upstairs, sir. They were all drunk. These photographs were on the floor.' The sergeant produced some pornographic photographs which portrayed people of different races mingling with each other in unlikely poses.

'How disgusting. Give them to me, Sergeant. We can't leave them here to corrupt the minds of the young.' The sergeant handed over the photographs to the inspector who smiled patronizingly at Joachim as he slipped them into his inside pocket.

'Let's go, Sergeant. Mrs Oak is not so simple as to believe that if she stops running our alsatians will not bite her.'

'Yes, sir.'

The policemen left, having done their duty. They had no intention of solving Vicky's problem. What they had done was to put the fear of God into Jenny Oak and convince Joachim that what Vicky had said about the house and its many inhabitants was true. Which was, of course, exactly what she had intended.

Joachim doubted Vicky's statements concerning the robbery as soon as he got back to bed and examined the events of the evening more critically. The cash-box and its ever-changing contents had existed, he was sure, only in her imagination.

None the less, in spite of his doubts, he signed a form for an insurance man the following morning, saying that he was prepared to testify, on oath if necessary, that Vicky had been feloniously robbed of a cash-box, containing two hundred and thirty-three pounds, ten shillings.

It was Christmas; she needed the money and, as he so often said, he hated insurance companies.

7

In spite of the cold wind and the heavy rain, Christine Murray was preparing to go out. It was ten days since she had sent Joachim off to church and no one had seen him since. He had not been near the university; neither Gerry nor Nick Hill had seen him and she was rather worried. It was not like him to go underground for so long. Some time ago he had promised to take her to the end-of-term party in the department of Sociology and Social Administration. That party was to take place this evening and, if they were going, arrangements must be made. She had decided, after waiting so long to hear from him, to go and visit him at his flat. He might be ill.

She wrapped her university scarf around her mouth and tucked it well inside her navy blue duffel coat, which she buttoned carefully all the way up. It was not far to his flat; she would be there in half an hour. He had said that there was a prostitute living on the ground floor so she had kept away from there until now. But if he was ill, and it seemed as if he might be, then she had a moral duty to go and see that he was being properly looked after, prostitute or not. She took her black woollen mittens from the drawer in the sideboard, turned off the gas fire, waited for it to pop before she put her hands into the mittens and left the room.

On her way downstairs she thought she should tell Mrs Richards that she was going out. It wasn't really necessary but Mrs Richards had been very kind to her lately, inviting her in for tea almost every morning since lectures finished. She knocked on Mrs Richards's door.

'I'm going out, Mrs Richards. I shouldn't be long.' She called through the closed door, her head inclined towards it at an angle of forty-five degrees. The door opened immediately.

'Did you say you were going out? In this weather? What on

earth for? It's pouring with rain. You'll catch your death of cold.' Mrs Richards was so overcome with concern that she allowed her mouth to remain open for several seconds after she had finished speaking. Christine smiled at her, consolingly.

'I shall be all right. I have to visit a sick friend or I wouldn't be going.'

'Well, make sure you wrap up well and don't catch cold. There's a lot of it about.'

'I am wrapped up well.' Christine stood in front of Mrs Richards like a well-scrubbed child waiting to have her hands inspected.

'Well you can't be too careful. Make sure you dry yourself out properly when you come home. In this weather you should have your fire on all the time.'

'You're just like my mother,' gurgled Christine, as she went to the front door.

She and Mrs Richards were getting along famously. She was sick of hearing complaints from other students at the university. They never stopped talking about how vicious and exploitative their landladies were. It seemed to her that the reason most of them fell out with their landladies was that they did not take any trouble to try to get on well with them. Landladies were human beings, with feelings, and if you treated them with consideration they would respond. There were bound to be exceptions, there were bound to be landladies who were in it for the money, but Mrs Richards was all right.

The average British cynic, like Joachim for example, would have laughed at Christine's analysis. Mrs Richards was as exploitative as the rest; her interest in Christine's health was selfish. By all means keep the fire on all the time; didn't she collect fifty per cent of the money which the tenants fed into their meters? And don't come back with a cold because you'll fill the house with germs. A house full of germs was followed by a sick husband, having to be nursed. Wrap up well and, if necessary, don't come back.

Christine pulled the cowl of her duffel coat over her head as she turned out of the garden into the street. The rain came at her in sharp circular gusts, driven by a wind, which had set off bombastically from the river, determined to get where it was going by the shortest possible route. But it had met some tall buildings on its journey, buildings which were too strong to remove and too tall to leap over. The wind, much to its displeasure, had been forced to follow the main roads through the centre of the city, channelled along them by the concrete strength of the department stores and insurance offices which stood shoulder to shoulder, like policemen at a royal procession, along the way. By the time the wind reached Christine it was frustrated beyond the point of endurance, having been buffeted from immovable object to immovable object. It dashed about in great anger, petulantly seizing anything it could master and throwing it high into the air and the driving rain. Old damp leaves twisted and curled in the showers, their decaying forms given a desperate new life, while cats, dogs and budgerigars disappeared from the streets to watch the proceedings in comfortable fear, from behind misty windows.

Christine was made of sterner stuff than the wind and the rain. She forced her way through them to the bus-stop without any sense of superiority, taking it for granted that, of all natural phenomena, she and her species were, at the same time, the most beautiful, the most powerful, and the most destructive.

There was a small queue at the bus-stop: six or seven people, two umbrellas and four shopping bags. They were a very miserable group, wet, cold and ill-tempered, having waited longer than they thought appropriate in this weather for a bus which cared not for their condition. They were complaining to each other as Christine attached herself to their tail. Wanting no part in their demonstration of ill-will she stuck her hands deep in the pockets of her coat inclining her head forward so that the rain would run off the cowl of her duffel coat into the gutter, where matchsticks and cigarette ends raced past her to the drain.

The bus journey was spoiled for her by a silly argument which developed between a woman and the bus-conductor, on the subject of the decline in relations between the bus service and its public. Soaked at the bus-stop and encouraged by the sympathetic hearing her complaints had received in the queue the woman had taken it upon herself to act as spokesman for the human race and had attacked the bus-conductor as he came for her fare.

'You were a long time coming,' she had said as he held out his hand for her money.

'Where are you going, missis?'

'To town. It's tenpence. Don't you realize that we were all soaked waiting for this bus? What were you doing, drinking tea?' She looked at her neighbour as she said this but her neighbour's support was not wholehearted, inhibited as it was by the proximity of the bus-conductor and the power of his uniform.

'It's a shilling, missis. And we're early. We weren't due at your stop till ten past and it's only ten past now.'

'It's tenpence. I'm not paying a shilling.'

'Well you'll have to get off. The fares went up on Monday.'

'I don't believe you.'

The bus-conductor rang the bell and the bus stopped at the side of the road.

'Come on. Off.' He jerked an authoritative thumb in the direction of the door. 'There's a policeman over there. Either you pay your fare or get off.'

The woman, having received no support from the former members of the bus queue, and having made a fool of herself by causing the bus to be stopped when no one wanted to get off or to get on, was forced to capitulate. Handing over her fare she made a final desperate attempt to restore her dignity. 'I shall report you to the Transport Department.'

The bus-conductor took out a pencil and a piece of paper, wrote out his service number, the number of the bus, the name of the driver, the time of day and handed it to the woman, demonstrating by this excess of melodramatic politeness the extreme weakness of the woman's case and his own lack of concern. 'Don't forget that this bus service is crying out for conductors,' he said as he handed it to her, 'the only reason they sack you is if you rape a passenger.'

And with that he had gone upstairs, leaving the woman to seek sympathy from the other passengers, a luxury which was bestowed while the bus-conductor was upstairs, but withdrawn abruptly as soon as he returned.

Christine got off the bus outside Joachim's flat. The rain had stopped, temporarily, having churned the wilderness of the bomb site into a thick swamp. She was not favourably impressed with the area Joachim had chosen to inhabit. If he was ill then it was not surprising, living as he did, in such a place. She walked up to the door of the house and knocked, even though it was open, and had obviously been open throughout the duration of the storm, to judge from the pile of leaves and the water in the porch. A letter from Littlewoods Pools swam in a corner on its own. She could see the postmark and the message from the G.P.O. in Liverpool encouraging everyone to post early for Christmas. The envelope was addressed to a Mrs Ball.

No one came to the door so Christine knocked again, this time harder and with more noise. She heard the sound of a door being unlocked and then the shuffle of feet in carpet slippers along the hall. A haggard woman, in a quilted housecoat and, presumably, her nightdress, opened the door.

'Does Mr Ryan live here?'

'Who?' Vicky was not very welcoming. She ignored

K

Christine's smile and her polite deference. It was cold, she had been dragged out of a warm dry bed and there had better be a good reason.

'Joachim Ryan. He works at the university in the Sociology . . .'

'Come in, will you, I'm freezing to death. He lives upstairs. He's probably still in bed, the lazy bugger.'

'Thank you. I'm sorry if I put you to any trouble.'

'I should think so. I've a few things to say to that bugger, inviting people round at all hours of the day and night. Shut that bloody door.'

Vicky had deduced that Christine was Joachim's girl-friend and this information did nothing to console her for being dragged out of bed. She made for Joachim's room and entered it without knocking. Joachim was not in bed, he was sitting in front of the fire in his pyjamas drinking coffee and smoking.

'Why don't you tell your friends where you live instead of getting me out of bed to let them in for you? What do you think I am, a bloody traffic warden?'

Joachim, about to pacify Vicky and to beseech her once more not to come into his room without knocking suddenly saw Christine, wet and shocked, standing inside the door. Before he could speak Vicky had turned her attention to Christine.

'Next time you come, love, just come straight in. I know why he makes me let you in; it's in case someone else gets here before you.'

She stormed downstairs leaving the two young people looking at each other, both of them very surprised and embarrassed.

'I'll get dressed,' said Joachim unnecessarily. 'Come over to the fire and take your things off.'

Christine stood rooted to the spot; she wasn't going to move until Joachim went to put some clothes on. He disappeared behind the hardboard screen and she began to feel better, though the water continued to drip from her clothes, on to the bare linoleum.

'Who was that awful woman?' she shouted over the screen. She was anxious to get to the fire but she was afraid to move in case she saw Joachim getting dressed. She was not acquainted with the geography of the flat, never having been there before. Nor did she know Joachim very well if she thought that he would be willing to dress and undress in front of her, as if she were his doctor.

'That was Vicky. Did she swear at you?' Joachim called back.

'Vicky the prostitute?'

'Yes.'

'How disgusting. Does she often come into your room without knocking?'

'All the time. She was never properly house-trained.'

Joachim emerged from behind the screen, having dressed very quickly. He waved Christine towards the fire. She was glad to accept his invitation and she stood in front of it, revelling in the heat. The steam spun out of her duffel coat in small clouds.

'Take your coat off and let it dry. I'll make you a cup of coffee.'

The embarrassment of the introduction was soon forgotten as the coffee was produced and consumed and as Christine settled down on the carpet in front of the fire.

'I thought you might be ill,' she said eventually, her eyes locked in the heart of the fire.

'Why? Because I have not been around the university?' Joachim knew that he was going to have to explain things to her eventually but he would welcome any distraction, any temporary tranquillizer.

'Yes, among other things. I came to see if you intended to take me to the party, as you promised.'

There was an unusual asperity in Christine's remark, born

possibly from the lack of warmth in Joachim's reception and from a certain jealousy of the ease with which a prostitute was admitted to his bedroom.

'Party?' Joachim had forgotten about the party. 'What party?'

'The end of term party in the department. You said you would take me. It's tonight.'

There was no way out; he would have to admit that he had forgotten all about it. He felt very guilty indeed.

'Hell, Christine, I'm sorry, I'd forgotten all about it. You see, we've had a lot of trouble here recently and I've not had much time to think about the department. We had a robbery last week and the police were all over the place. Then they came to take Gordon away but he gave them the slip.'

Christine listened while Joachim fabricated his story from the events of the previous ten days. He was skilful and his explanation was accepted, not because it was plausible, but because Christine wanted to believe it. She had been shaken by Vicky's remark about other people getting to Joachim first. She had never considered the possibility that he might be growing disenchanted; his protestations about involvement and about honesty in relationships had left her in no doubt that he was much taken with her and that he was sincere in seeking her affection. He had reprimanded her often enough because she was not prepared to return this goodwill by gestures of her own, and he had made her feel very guilty, because she was fond of him and would have been delighted to be able to show this, had she known how, and had she not been too afraid. So she believed his explanation, she believed that the reason he had not seen her was that he had been too busy with problems in this house. But she saw, for the first time, that their relationship was in danger of crumbling and she was very frustrated, because she did not know what to do about it.

Joachim, ineptly warding off the evil hour, arranged to take her to the party in the staff common room in the department. He did not want to go to the party, and he was surprised to discover that his interest in her, which he had decided to kill off because he had felt like a leper in the company of a child, was now disappearing of its own accord, guided no doubt by those same intangible forces which had aroused it in the first place. Having sought her and impressed her he saw that he could never love her and as love was the Prime Mover in everything he saw himself doing, the relationship must end. When and how and where were tactical problems.

She left him, regretting that she had decided to come to his flat and without asking him what Vicky had meant in her remarks about finding that others might have got to his room first. They had arranged to meet in the department at eight that evening and they parted with that prospect in mind. For Joachim it was to be the first step in his campaign to divest himself of her, for Christine it was to be the beginning of her campaign to retain him. With such diverse aims and purposes bound up in the same evening one of them had to lose and to suffer.

On her way home she stopped off at a chemist's to buy bath salts, false eyelashes, and perfume. That afternoon she asked Hazel Nutt to set her hair and to help her choose a dress for the party. Like many women before her she had learned that the maintenance of good relations between men and women owed as much to the tactical exploitation of limited resources as it did to animal magnetism. With all the armour the cosmetics industry could supply at her disposal she chose her weapons carefully and with Hazel's courage modified by her own common sense she prepared herself well. No one would be able to ignore her this evening.

She had never been a huntress before; the experience was not something she could encounter in terms of the rules of politeness and schoolgirl decorum which she was accustomed to employ in the solution of her other problems. For the first time in her life she was forced to operate outside these rules. Until now she had subjected Joachim to these rules, reprimanding him when he transgressed them, awarding him merit marks when his behaviour fell into the categories they created. Nice boys knew the rules and obeyed them. Joachim was not nice, in terms of the rules; everything she knew about him fell outside their narrow boundaries. He lived in the same house as a prostitute with whom he seemed to get on very well; nice boys avoided prostitutes. He never went to church, which was bad enough in a Protestant but in a man who had been educated at a good Catholic Public school it was disgraceful. He smoked too much, drank too much and swore, he was bad tempered, selfish, and sometimes lewd. He was lazy and cynical, attacking her every belief, religious, political and social. Yet he could also be kind and sympathetic and he was honest.

The rules did not apply to Joachim; if she was to catch him she would have to put her campaign on a much sounder basis than middle-class etiquette. She would have to try to see the situation from his point of view, try to understand what he wanted from her and whether she would keep him by giving it to him. The rules fell away like rotten cabbage leaves as she struggled to reach the heart of the matter.

For the first time in her life too, she was forced to consider the possibility of sexual intercourse. Ever since her schooldays, when the nun who had taught them the Social Policies of the Church had said that only men took pleasure in sex and that women had to endure it in pain to compensate for the joys of motherhood, she had never wanted to go to bed with a man. She had not believed the nun – after all nuns couldn't really be expected to know all that much about it and some of the girls in her class at school had said that they had found the experience thoroughly pleasing – but she had retained the image because it had powerfully described her own fears.

She had reprimanded Hazel time and again, because Hazel would never talk about anything but sex and was always wishing herself away in the naked arms of some man she had encountered at the bus-stop or at the poetry reading circle. Hazel treated sex as if it were a marvellous toy she had been given for her birthday. For Christine the rules and conditions had been laid down very clearly by Pope Pius XII in his encyclicals *Casta Connubi* and *Sacra Virginitas*. Sexual intercourse, a pleasurable activity, designed by God, was confined to marriage, it had two purposes: the procreation of children and the expression of mutual love and anyone who sought to prevent the procreation of children by artificial and unnatural devices was punishable by spiritual death. No partner could refuse the other's demand to engage in sexual intercourse and the contract of marriage, though spiritual and sacramental, gave each partner the right to a monopoly of the other's body. Marriage was not an inferior state, but virginity was better.

Her virginity was a terrible price to have to pay for Joachim. He might not want it; he would know what her own inhibitions were, having read the same encyclicals and done the same compulsory sixth form course in Catholic Social Policy as herself. But he had said, often enough, that the Catholic Church in the twentieth century had issued statement after statement in which it had demonstrated that it knew less about sex than the early christians. Sex was love, he had said, and he couldn't have the one without the other. What she had to decide, if she intended to pursue her campaign to its conclusion was whether she was going to take him at his word. Would she, if he asked her, go to bed with him?

Joachim, having been to bed with Jenny Oak, had decided that he could not love Christine Murray. At first his decision arose from his share in the old-fashioned puritan ethic of arriving brand new at the marital bed, but lately he had convinced himself that he could not love Christine Murray because he had never loved her. He had been fooling himself, let himself be seduced by her innocence and by her stubborn resistance to his charm. Looked at in the dim damp dungeon light of his cut-price bedsitter, their relationship was seen to be a sequence of accidental encounters between two people with nothing in common, saying nothing to each other, sharing nothing beyond a ride on a bus or a visit to the same cinema on the same evening.

There was no logic in his analysis. His present attitude had been sparked off by his night in bed with Jenny Oak, but Jenny Oak was not his first seducer, so that, without her, he would still have arrived at Christine's bedroom tainted with the memories of other sheets and other ejaculations. But logic has little to do with these affairs. Logic involves responsibility and obligations when a man as moral as Joachim allows it to dominate his thinking. He could not afford to be logical about Christine Murray. It seemed that she was growing fond of him and he had encouraged her to develop in this direction. Logically, he was responsible for her attitude to him; logically, it was his fault that she was falling in love with him. But she had to go.

Men who start wars often flee the scene before the war burns itself out; it was that way with Joachim. Wars and love affairs are savage monsters and it is rare that the men responsible for their outbreak cope successfully with their conclusion. Much the easiest solution is to run away.

Joachim left his flat at six o'clock that evening. He had arranged to meet Christine in the department at eight but he wanted to visit the pub before then. He had arranged to meet her rather than call for her at her flat because he wanted to impress her with his indifference and to demolish those attitudes towards him which he had worked so hard to put up. He also intended to arrive at his tryst as drunk as possible.

Gerry was in the pub when he got there. Joachim saw him as

soon as he pushed through the half open door. He was sitting at the bar on a high stool, his head supported in his hands. He was brooding over a pint of beer and he looked very miserable. Joachim walked up behind him, resisting the urge to slap him in the middle of the back, as any hearty worth the name would certainly have done.

'Hello, Gerry,' was the greeting he settled for, delivering it quietly so as not to alarm the man too much, 'you don't look very happy.'

Gerry turned to look at Joachim. He didn't smile too well but there was some indication in his change of expression that he was pleased to see him. 'Evening, Joachim, would you like a drink?' He put his hand into his pocket and pulled out some loose change.

'I'll have a pint of bitter please, Gerry.'

The pint of bitter was ordered and delivered. While he was waiting for it Joachim looked around him at the few occupants of the almost empty pub. It was too early for the young trendies, who arrived to pack the place an hour before closing time. The scene was depressingly sober and damp. Two men stood alone at the bar, their hands deep in their pockets, their eyes staring directly in front of them, lost on some fantastic trip to wonderland. In one corner a dapper young salesman in a hand-cut suit was impressing two middle-aged clients with his displays of wit and provincial *savoir-faire*. Two sailors, having learned that this was the pub in which they could catch the trendy parties, had arrived too early. They talked to each other in a corner by the door, uncomfortable and incongruous. Joachim was tempted to tell them that they didn't stand a chance of mingling with the beautiful people. The trendies hated all uniforms but their own. The sailors would not have thanked him for this information.

'Thanks, Gerry. Cheers.' Joachim lifted the glass to his lips and drank three or four mouthfuls before replacing it on the bar. In the south of England they put handles on their pints of bitter; here the men preferred to drink from milk bottles.

'That girl was looking for you the other day.' Gerry had returned to gazing into his pint of beer; he offered this piece of information mechanically as if he had been programmed to submit it as a start to a conversation.

'She found me. Are you going to this party tonight?'

'Which party? The one in the department?'

'The one in the department.' Joachim tried to stir Gerry into taking a more active part in the conversation.

'Might as well. We're paying for it.'

'Who is?'

'We are. You and me and the rest of the staff. It was Nickill's idea. Said the staff should treat the students at the end of term. It's going to cost us about three pounds each.'

'Is he in charge of the funds?'

'He's in charge of everything. He's booked a pop group, ordered the drinks, and his girl-friend made the butties.'

'Then he can wait for my money.'

'He's already got it. He arranged with Serendipity to have it deducted from everyone's salary. Said it saved tax.'

'The cheeky bastard.'

'He'll probably be promoted. Serendipity liked the idea and Nickill probably didn't charge him. That's the way to get on.'

Gerry left his stool to go to the Gents. When he returned he was as miserable as he had been when Joachim had walked into the pub.

'Is anything wrong?' Joachim asked him, rendered impotent by the depth of such depression.

'No more than usual. My latest attempt to escape the savage clutches of academic life has met with the fate encountered by all its predecessors.'

Joachim was impressed by this sudden outburst of grammar from a man who had done nothing but spit sharp statements into his beer all evening but it did not explain why Gerry was feeling miserable.

'How?' Was the word Joachim chose to help clarify the situation without giving offence.

Gerry reached into the inside pocket of his jacket and pulled out a piece of notepaper which he handed to Joachim without speaking. The message was on the paper; presumably it would explain everything. It was a letter from a television company.

Dear Mr Shakespeare,

We have now had a chance to consider your play 'Babble On' and I must return it with regret that it wasn't liked enough for production to be offered.

There doesn't seem to us to be enough style and precision to redeem the vague technique or the rather extravagantly large cast, some of whom have no real place in the action.

I am sorry to have to write so disappointingly.

Yours sincerely,
Evelyn Beam

Senior Assistant
Script Unit.

'Who's this fellow Shakespeare?' Joachim asked, trying to make sense of the letter.

'Me. It's a pseudonym I use to make sure they read my stuff. Sometimes they send the stuff back without looking at it. With a name like Shakespeare they're bound to read it, just in case.'

'You're wasting your time, Gerry.'

'Thanks.'

'I don't mean your writing is bad. I don't know what it's like; I've never seen any of it.'

'Give yourself a treat. This is a piece I wrote last week on the subject of the delusions of grandeur shared by every sociologist I know.' Gerry handed Joachim an envelope. Joachim was about to open it but Gerry stopped him.

'Not now. Wait till you get home.'

'What I meant was – Come on we'll have another drink, you're empty – what I meant was that you'll never get anything accepted if you stay up here. The mandarins won't let you.'

'What bloody mandarins?'

'The literary élite in London. They have a little office in the National Gallery. I met one once in the Gents there. He was wearing a pointed hat and a pinafore borrowed from the Freemasons. Nobody can do anything without the mandarins. They run everything: the colour supplements, book reviews, publishing, television, the theatre, films, art galleries, exhibitions, concerts and rumour has it that they're moving into football. With the mandarins behind you the streets of London are paved with gold. They control it all, huddled together in the basement of the National Gallery. If you want to make it, get down there and start paying your tithes.'

Gerry laughed, grasping the point of Joachim's fairy tale.

'Look at this bird Evelyn Beam.' Joachim waved the letter in front of Gerry's nose.

'She can't write for toffee and there she is dismissing stuff like yours every day. She must be in with the mandarins. In fact I shouldn't be surprised if she was one of them.'

'True enough, she can't write, but then she doesn't have to. She's a rejector and it's much easier to reject a new play and send it back to the author than it is to accept one and justify it to the people who are going to put up the money to produce it.'

'Exactly. The only way to impress people like her is to get yourself a name. Borrowing someone else's won't get you any-

where. The only way to get a name is to go and see the mandarins. They control names.'

The beer arrived and both of them paused to refresh themselves, drinking from their glasses in unison. They were arming
up for one of those intense conversations which was supposed
to distinguish this pub from most of the others in the city. The
sailors at the door watched them with amusement.

The rain had stopped by the time Christine was ready to
leave for the party so that she was able to dispense with the
services of her hardy duffel coat. Instead she wore her snug
feminine green mohair coat with a dark blue silk scarf and a
cheeky Tam O' Shanter in the harlot tartan of the Royal Stu-
arts. Hazel had persuaded her to wear a very short white caftan
dress, with pale stocking tights and navy pants. Hazel had deduced from the poems of the local hippies, that there was nothing which stimulated a young man to thoughts of love more
than a glimpse of schoolgirl knickers. Christine accepted her
suggestion because navy blue was the colour of her shoes and
as her pants were as likely to be as much on view as her shoes
she did not want the colours to clash. She did not believe Hazel's
theory that there is nothing more sexy than innocence.

She took a taxi to the university, arriving at the department
five minutes after the time Joachim had said he would be there.
She paid the driver and walked slowly up the steps leading into
the entrance hall, confident that she looked her best, protected
by the ride in the taxi from any mischief the elements might
have done her. She opened the door, smiled at the porter who
was working overtime very unwillingly and looked around the
entrance hall to see if she could find Joachim among the many
young men who were standing there, waiting for their partners
to come out of the ladies' cloakroom. He was not there.

So she went to join the other girls in the ladies' cloakroom,
quite sure that, by the time she came out, he would have arrived and would be waiting for her. There was nothing to do

in the ladies' cloakroom. Other girls, who had not prepared themselves as carefully as she had done, were busy with the bits and pieces of making up their faces and adjusting their underwear. All she could do was comb her hair for ten minutes. She locked up her coat and scarf and tam-o'-shanter, took up a position in front of the mirror and combed her hair until she was sure he must be outside.

But he was not waiting for her when she came out of the ladies' cloakroom. She had to stand in the cold entrance hall, shivering with embarrassment, while the traffic flowed past her up the stairs to the staff common room. It was wicked of Joachim to leave her like this. If he was going to be late he should have 'phoned her at Mrs Richards'. It wasn't fair to make her stand in that cold hall, the only girl in a room full of waiting men, all of them staring at her and mentally stripping her of the few clothes she was wearing.

Quentin Tumble, having attended the party for half an hour, was about to leave the building when he noticed Christine standing alone in the entrance hall. He recognized her as Ryan's girl-friend and he reminded himself that she was very pretty. She seemed to him to be distressed at something. He decided to go over to her to see what he could do. She must be waiting for Ryan, who was probably in the Gents.

Christine saw him coming over. She knew him as Joachim's eccentric boss. The only thing eccentric about him this evening was his suit, which reminded her of a photograph she had seen on the cover of a recent edition of the *Radio Times*. It was bottle-green, with a long jacket with four buttons and short lapels, narrow trousers without turnups, and no waistcoat. It was very elegant.

'Are you waiting for Ryan?' Tumble called out as he came over.

Christine assumed that Tumble knew where Joachim was and that he was coming over to explain why her beloved had been delayed. This pleased her so much that she greeted Tumble with a smile so warm that he interpreted it incorrectly, taking it as a compliment to himself and his suit.

'Yes?' she replied cheerfully. 'Have you seen him?'

'I'm afraid not. When I saw you I thought he must be here.'

Christine was disappointed and resumed the expression of misery which had brought Tumble over from the other side of the hall. He saw an opportunity to comfort her.

'I'm sure he won't be long. He's a very reliable young man.' He stood back, waiting for the magic in the words to take effect.

'Yes.' She nodded sadly.

'Look. Why don't you go upstairs and wait for him there.'

'If he doesn't arrive in the next five minutes I'm going home.'

Tumble looked at her very carefully. If Ryan was not here then he probably wasn't coming and this innocent girl, who had prepared herself for an evening of dancing and love, would be left stranded, her preparations wasted, her spirits destroyed and her sacrifice postponed. If he was willing to exert himself he could take her to the party and take advantage of her disappointment when she realized that Ryan was not going to arrive. It might not work, but, as long as he was discreet, he had nothing to lose.

'Well, I must go back upstairs. When I saw you I was on my way out but you reminded me of my responsibilities. In spite of Mr Nick Hill and his persecutions I must remain at this party. If only to protect innocent students from his lunatic plans for them.'

Christine had learned all about Nick Hill from Joachim and she had met the gentleman herself often enough to know why all his friends disliked him. She didn't want to go upstairs without Joachim but neither did she want to be left down here on her own.

'What is he doing?' she asked, giggling pleasantly to keep Tumble there.

'He has filled the common room with barrels of cheap and stale beer and when I left he was walking round the room with a thurifer, choking everyone with smoke and what he called incense.'

'You mean a thurible. A thurifer is someone who swings a thurible.'

Tumble bowed his head, wishing to indicate humility in the face of such expert knowledge. Christine laughed.

'Are you sure you will not come upstairs with me; you could protect me from Hill until Ryan arrives?'

Christine looked at the door of the building which had remained firmly closed throughout her conversation with Tumble. If Joachim was coming he might not be here for a long time. One thing was clear; he was not just late. He had obviously been delayed, perhaps because he had not wanted to come at all, perhaps by that prostitute woman. But he would come eventually. When he did he would be feeling very guilty and that would make things much easier for her. 'Yes, I will. It's cold down here.'

It was not cold in the pub where Joachim and Gerry were being pushed steadily against the bar by the group of young trendies behind them. They preferred to remain at the bar because it was the only place in the pub where they could be sure of maintaining a regular supply of beer. They were both quite drunk, but their dedication to their conversation had distracted them from the passage of time and they had not counted their drinks. The trendies were talking clothes and trying to avoid buying the round of beer.

Gerry had explained why he was so miserable. He had, for some time, expected that one or other of his pieces would be accepted by a literary journal. His television play had been his most ambitious project so far. Had it been taken he would have received a large sum of money, enough to make it possible for him to escape from the department of Sociology and Social Administration. The television company had held his play for six weeks, tormenting him into believing that it was under careful consideration, that it was being passed on from expert to expert, its every epigram enjoyed and noted. When it was returned, summarily dismissed, with no indication it had been read, his dreams were shattered. Joachim had laughed at Gerry's innocence. Why should he assume that television companies were less corrupt than other businesses? And who were these experts they were supposed to employ? Didn't Gerry know by now that there were no experts in the world of bureaucratic art, only myopes in positions of power.

If Gerry wanted to liberate himself from the university by this means then there were two main courses of action open to him. He could achieve national fame by performing some heroic and completely irrelevant feat of endurance or bravery, like swimming the Atlantic or climbing Everest from the inside. This done, the nation and its publishers and editors would grovel at his feet. As soon as it was discovered that he had the remotest literary talent his every grunt and groan would be published in hardback and in paperback, serialized by the Sunday papers, documented by the B.B.C., in every possible form and from every possible angle shovelled on to a willing public.

The second course of action was more difficult and less sure of success. It involved ingratiating himself with the mandarins. This is much easier if one starts as an undergraduate at Oxford but for Gerry it would mean that he would have to spend hours hanging around the basement of the National Gallery, trying to learn the passwords.

Joachim's humour did nothing to exorcise Gerry's depression but it provided some justification for the process

L

of rationalization he had to adopt so as to adapt himself to the tragedy of the rejection of his play. He found it much easier to accept the dismissal of the play when he convinced himself that the cause lay in the system. His literary mettle unchallenged and untarnished, he could relax a little and get drunk.

The group of trendies had finished their peacock dance. One of them, having been forced by the meanness of the others to buy the round of beer which would last them all night, forced his way between Gerry and Joachim.

'Six halves of bitter,' he called out to the barman, expecting the man to wilt at the prospect of having to supply such an order. He was disappointed. The barman ignored him, reserving his attention for the dapper salesman, who was still impressing his middle-aged clients in the corner of the bar. The salesman had already invested three pounds ten shillings in drinks and tips; pretty soon there would be a deal clinched, a celebration round and a huge gratuity for the man who provided that round. As a customer the narcissistic trendy was last.

'Why are you so eager to leave the department?' Joachim asked Gerry, leaning back so that his words could travel behind the waiting trendy, who was still standing between them.

'Because it's frustrating.'

'Is that all?'

'Perhaps we see the situation from different vantage points. After all you're never in the bloody place,' Gerry shouted back, startling the trendy with his outburst of aggression.

'True. Would it be less frustrating for you if you didn't have to get up so early in the morning?'

'Yes. But I should still leave.'

'Why?'

'Because I can see no purpose in what goes on. When I took a job in a university I was trying to escape from industry where a man is successful over the dead bodies of his friends. I thought that university life was free from that sort of thing.' Gerry, having found another reason for being miserable, resumed his contemplation of his glass of beer.

'You make the mistake of judging the quality of a university by looking at the rituals of its common room. The only criterion to adopt, in a university like ours, is the library. The quality of our university lies in the quality of its library. Other universities sometimes employ creative geniuses; we don't. It's all a product of supply and demand. Geniuses are rare; they tend to go to the best universities.'

At this point the young trendy was visited by the barman who gave him his beer. Gerry and Joachim were left alone.

'I wasn't complaining about the lack of geniuses. I was complaining about the lack of humanity. I was indoctrinated with the idea that sociology was a humanistic discipline, that it bred idealists and reformers. I did not expect the department to be what I found it to be, a cattle market, where ideals are bought and sold for promotion and favour.'

'So you are leaving.'

'I don't know. I can't leave without having somewhere to go. I don't think there is anywhere to go.'

'Well then. You might as well stay here and make the most of it. In the eyes of the world you have a good job. No one ever asks you to do any work.'

Gerry looked up from his beer to stare at the bottles of spirits suspended upside down in front of the mirrors. In the mirrors he could see the group of young people behind him. They were talking in monosyllables about this and that, using words which were given to them by the leaders of the clothes-conscious, drug happy, pop song world they had chosen to call their own. He decided to give them a sentence to think about.

'A tumbler of poisoned water may be termed "good" in that it will satisfy any man's animal thirst, but if he drinks it, it will not be good for him.'

'In the same way that the pursuit of a good is not always the same thing as good behaviour,' Joachim contributed, seeing Gerry's game.

'I disagree, good behaviour is always behaviour in pursuit of a good. But the good pursued may be evil and that makes the behaviour both evil and good.'

'Very good,' laughed Joachim. 'St Thomas has made scholars of us both.'

'Not scholars. Scholastics.'

Unfortunately the young people behind them had ignored their clever conversation. As soon as the first sentence was uttered they had stopped listening; they were not interested in playing with words. They had more important things to do.

'Shall we go and have a look at this party?' Gerry asked, suddenly growing tired of the pub. It would soon be invaded by narcissistic teenagers, their sweaty armpits caked with talcum powder and sprayed with deodorant, the twin gods of the sixties neurotic.

'If you like. I said I would meet Christine there.'

The two philosophers drank their beer, visited the gents, and left the pub by a side door. As they walked towards the university they came upon groups of pubescent girls waiting in the cold night for their boy-friends to arrive and take them into the pub. Gerry and Joachim smiled at the girls and passed on.

'Would you like another drink?' Tumble bent over Christine who was sitting on a chair in the corner of the common room. They had been dancing to the pop group which was now taking a rest in the corner farthest away from them.

'Yes, please.' Christine looked up and smiled, pleasing Tumble more than she knew.

The party was not nearly as bad as Tumble had described. Nick Hill had provided a pop group which had kept the students dancing and the sandwiches and drinks were plentiful and easy on the palate. For some time she had been ill at ease, with half an eye on the door looking for Joachim. But Tumble had been very sweet. He had not taken her over to the corner where the rest of the staff were sitting, realizing that she would have been very uncomfortable among them. Instead he had allowed her to go where she wanted, protecting her when she went to collect sandwiches, dancing with her whenever she wanted to dance and fetching her a drink when she was thirsty. There was something about him which reminded her of her father. It was probably his age or his maturity. Whatever it was she felt very secure with him, and very grateful: he didn't have to stay here with her. She was sure he must prefer to be elsewhere, doing something more to his taste.

Tumble returned with the drinks. Christine had said that she preferred shandy but he had persuaded her that Nick Hill's beer was unhygienic so that she was now about to consume her fifth vodka-with-orange, which was more in keeping with his plans than shandy. She seemed to have forgotten about Ryan.

Christine sipped her drink slowly. She would have preferred a long cool drink because she felt hot after the dancing. But it had been nice of Tumble to fetch this for her and she must be polite to him. She watched the patterns of light moving across the wall opposite. Nick Hill had installed a projector behind the bar. It was throwing moving shapes of yellow and green light across the room, sometimes catching people unawares and turning them into fairies and hobgoblins. It was very pleasant to sit here and watch it all. It made one think of magic and wizards and gingerbread men.

She surrendered to a gentle hiccup and giggled. She was quite drunk already. She mustn't have any more or she would be sick. She had never been drunk before, not really drunk, that is. Once in Italy, she had taken two glasses of white wine which had set her giggling all night. Daddy had said that if she ever did it again he would put her over his knee so every summer since then she had pretended to be drunk to tease him. Once he had chased her along the beach in Venice but he couldn't catch her.

Tumble watched Christine hiccup and chuckle and dream. From where he was looking she had the appearance of a very young, very innocent schoolgirl. He was reminded of Jenny Oak's remark in Oily Johnnys when she had told him that he ought to marry such a girl. He was not too old for her, not according to Aristotle who preached that the ideal marriage was one which took place between a man of thirty-seven and a girl of seventeen. What would marriage be like with Christine? Pleasant, certainly, because she was young and beautiful. Safe, because she would heed his word in all matters; and comfortable, because she wanted nothing from him that he was not prepared to give freely.

He lapsed into dreaming, gazing fondly on her as his thoughts wandered into the future. Christine continued to look at the moving shadows on the wall and the two of them remained as still and serene as an Edwardian photograph, lost in the soft colours of their dreams. Neither saw Joachim and Gerry come in through the door; neither saw Nick Hill walk over to his tardy guests, his thurible swinging over them in ceremonious welcome.

It was the pop group which shook them. A tumultuous roll on the drums shattered their serenity. The languid room quickened with the irritation, not at all pleased at the sudden departure of the spell the moving light had worked over them all. Christine jerked forward at the crash, spilling some of her drink on the floor. Then she saw Joachim receiving a glass of beer at the bar.

She jumped out of her chair, amusing some of the people near her who thought she had been frightened by the noise of the drums. She forgot the tactics she had worked out when she had been waiting for him in the entrance hall. She had resigned herself to the notion that he might not come at all, that he might have been waylaid by that prostitute woman. But he was here and his arrival was like peace at the end of war; it made her want to cry out to him and dance with relief. She walked over towards him, tottering a little with the drink in her. Behind her was Tumble who had seen Joachim at the bar. He was not as happy with the arrival as Christine.

'Joachim, where have you been? I thought you were never coming.'

Joachim turned from the bar to look at Christine. She was a little drunk and her eyes were wet and crazy. She raised a hand to touch his shoulder and then withdrew it quickly, indicating in that one gesture that she loved him and feared him. Fear, apparently, was the stronger emotion. He felt some pity for her, pity and lust, because she looked ravishingly beautiful; but the pity was transient and the lust heavy with guilt. If he must do it he must do it quickly. He must divest himself of her tonight.

'I'm sorry, Christine. I'm a little drunk.' He said this coldly, with no emotion.

'Are you? So am I.' Christine forgot that she was supposed to reprimand him for being late.

'Your young lady was about to go home, Ryan, but I persuaded her to wait for you up here.' Tumble intervened, reminding Christine that she had been abused and Joachim that he had been impolite.

'Thanks very much. She should have gone home.'

Christine saw this statement as the culmination of all she had feared. She did not burst into tears, though she wanted to very much. Instead she turned to Tumble very stiffly.

'He is right, Mr Tumble. I should go home. Thank you very much for looking after me.' She put her glass down on the bar and then ran from the room as fast as she could, leaving Joachim and Tumble to look at each other.

'That was most unchivalrous of you, Ryan.' Tumble was annoyed at what seemed to be the sudden dissolution of his plans for the evening.

'Then rescue the damsel yourself, Sir Quentin. Take her home in your car.'

Tumble left the room without speaking. Of course he would take her home. Ryan had placed her fairly in his charge, exactly as he wanted. If she declined his offer he would insist, saying that she was in no condition to travel through the city on her own. Joachim watched him leave and then turned to finish his glass of beer, grateful beyond measure that it had been so easy.

He was joined by Gerry, who had been to the lavatory again in response to the authority of his bladder, which was small and incapable of coping with excesses of liquid.

'Let us fill some tankards and withdraw to a corner, there to continue the argument concerning good and evil,' he suggested. The alcohol in him was working hard, rendering his speech melodramatic and formal.

'Our argument on good and evil was false, being based on licensed premises,' replied Joachim calmly, indicating that his reading had not been entirely confined to paperback novels of indolent lust. Gerry missed the plagiarism but he understood the joke. While he laughed they filled six large tumblers with beer and retired to a corner of the room, where they could sit and abuse the activities of the others in the room.

'I see that there are several bottles of good whiskey hidden in brown boxes behind the bar,' Joachim observed, between sips of beer.

'Then we must remove some to another place. We cannot allow Nickill to fall into temptation. We must protect him from his greed, and this assembly from the corruption of its organizers.' Gerry leaned back on his chair, throwing two unsteady legs on to a table in front of him.

'Agreed.' Joachim assumed a posture as languid as his companion's. 'Fiat.'

The rain had returned. It pursued Tumble's car all the way to Christine's flat, providing the travellers with timely distraction from the problem of thinking of words to say to each other. Except for the noise of the rain on the roof and the tireless motion of the windscreen wipers the journey was taken in silence. When the car stopped outside the house there was a dampness in the air-conditioning, a cold presence which cut short the processes of perspiration and removed the smell of clothes drying on hot bodies.

'Thank you, Mr Tumble.' Christine looked for the door handle. She wanted to run into the house, lock herself in her room and lie on her bed in solitary misery.

'You are welcome, Christine.' Tumble remained as he was, making no move to help her open the door. If she was not going to invite him in for a drink of something then he must invite himself.

'I'm afraid you've had a very boring evening. I should have come straight home when Joachim didn't turn up. It was good of you to look after me.'

'Not at all. I enjoyed the party and I enjoyed looking after you, as you put it. But if it will make you feel less guilty I will allow you to offer me a reward. If you give me a cup of coffee I shall absolve you of all obligation.'

'Are you thirsty? I'm sorry. I am being very impolite. Of course you may have a cup of coffee.' Christine thought about Mrs Richards's rules about men but surely they did not apply to university lecturers.

'I am not thirsty but I should like some coffee, partly to make sure that you are safe and sound and partly to avoid the possibility of failing one of those police breath tests. This rain makes driving difficult and I am sure I have had more alcohol than the law allows.' He leaned over Christine's lap while he opened the car door for her. She lay back in her seat to give him access to the handle, unwittingly revealing most of her white stockings.

Christine's room was warm with the welcome of the gas fire which had been burning all the time she had been at the party. Tumble shook himself as he came through the door.

'This is a warm room,' he said. 'I wish my flat were as warm as this.'

'Sit down then and enjoy it while I make the coffee.'

'Thank you.' Tumble stretched out in the armchair, exposing as much of his body as possible to the fire. In this and in every involuntary action he had produced since he had entered the room he was giving a very good charade of a wet sheepdog at his master's hearth. When Christine came back with the coffee she was offered the choice of sitting on the floor or on the bed. She sat on the bed.

Mrs Richards's many wooden clocks chimed the hour in philistine cacophony in the hall. Eleven o'clock. Well that was one rule gone. She would have to explain to Mrs Richards tomorrow that the man in her room was a university lecturer, not a boy-friend.

'Are you a Catholic, Christine?' Tumble asked, pulling a small pipe from his pocket. He did not look directly at her: she was sitting on the bed which was behind him, to his left.

'Yes.' Christine was tired. Would he think she was impolite if she took off her shoes and lay on the bed. Perhaps he wouldn't notice. He couldn't see her from the armchair.

'I thought so. Your remark about the thurible was obviously a piece of inside information.'

'The Catholic church does not have a monopoly of the use of thuribles and incense.'

She was being impolite again. Why was it that non-Catholics always looked on her and her fellow Catholics as freaks, as if they were governed by different forces, living lives quite different from the rest of mankind?

'I am continually fascinated by the Catholic heritage. As you know, my main area of interest in Sociology is in courtship patterns. I once prepared a conference paper entitled "Frigidity and Clerical Control in the West of Ireland" and my research involved me in a detailed study of Thomas Aquinas and Sean O'Casey. It was a most interesting part of my life – no one could tell me where sexual behaviour was good and where it was evil.'

Tumble was wasting his time. Christine had closed her eyes on the bed and was hardly listening. It did not matter; he insisted on making his point. 'Aquinas, for instance, who was clearer than most of his contemporaries, was forced to conclude that sex was an evil but not a sin, which was a distinction I could never understand.' He puffed his pipe and relaxed, waiting for the effect this piece of irrelevant scholarship would have on an audience which wasn't even listening. After a long silence he was forced to continue. 'I suppose he thought it was evil because it is an activity which is carnal, man behaving as an animal, the rational faculty completely submerged. It could not be sinful because it was the only means known at the time of propagating the species.'

Christine suddenly thought how odd it was for this man to be discussing sex in so clinical a fashion when that morning she had subjected herself to a personal inquiry on the same subject. She had not been so objective. She had anticipated a more personal involvement and had the evening taken a more favourable course she might not be alone on this bed now. One thing was certain: Joachim would never be the same again. Even if he were to come round in the morning to apologize and crave her affection she could not give it to him. He would never know the sacrifice she had almost made.

'You haven't been listening.' Tumble had risen from his armchair and was now standing by the bed wagging a finger in admonition.

'I'm sorry.' Christine began to get off the bed, guilty at having to be reminded that she had a guest whom she was neglecting.

'Don't get up.' Tumble put a hand on her shoulder. She lay down again quickly.

'You're not afraid of me, are you?' Tumble asked her. It would be easier if she were afraid of him. He could take her hand in his, stroke it tenderly, whisper soft practised words of reassurance.

'No. I feel perfectly safe. Why should you frighten me?'

Tumble had never frightened any woman in his life. A young girl should be easy to frighten. All the women he had known had played with him, had done what they wanted with him. He was not taking this from a young girl.

'Why do you think I am here?' He sat on the bed beside her, purposefully, with a coolness which surprised him.

Christine looked at him as if he were a ghost from Hell. What did he mean? Surely he was not trying to seduce her. Not Tumble. He was a lecturer. She had admitted him to her flat in that role: she was a student, he a lecturer and their relationship was defined clearly. Lecturers don't seduce students. They teach them, give them advice, lend them money, but they don't go to bed with them.

'So. You are afraid of me.' There was triumph in Tumble's voice. He was like a boy pulling the wings off his first butterfly. He grasped Christine's hand which settled in his own without feeling.

This was monstrous. It was like going to confession and finding the priest's hand up your skirt. Christine sat up.

'I did not expect this. I have only thought of you as a lecturer.'

'Being a lecturer does not stop me from being a man. As a man I find you an extremely attractive woman.'

'I'll make some coffee.' Christine got up from the bed to run to the kitchen, there to compose herself. As she went out of the room she could hear Mrs Richards at the front door. She must have seen Tumble's car.

'Is that you, Miss Murray?' Mrs Richards had heard Christine moving from her living-room to her kitchen. Her tone was formal, remonstrative, offended.

'Yes, Mrs Richards.'

'Do you know anything about the car at the front of the house?'

'It belongs to a visitor of mine.'

'Then it should not be there. It's past the time for visitors.'

'I know. He will be going soon.'

'He?'

'He is a lecturer from the university. He isn't a boy-friend.'

'That is no excuse. My visiting times apply to all men, particularly university lecturers. They're just as bad as the rest. There was a play on the television about a university lecturer last night. I shall speak to you in the morning.'

'Yes, Mrs Richards.'

Christine heard a door close noisily at the bottom of the stairs and assumed that Mrs Richards had gone back into her part of the house. She went into her own kitchen to make the coffee.

Tumble had not altered his campaign to suit the changing circumstances. When she gave him his coffee he grasped her hand, holding it as long as he could without spilling his drink. Christine reflected that perhaps this was how the men with experience went about it. She was very confused.

All day she had been preparing herself for bed. Unwillingly without knowing what she was going through she had considered the possibility that Joachim might try to seduce her and that she might allow him to do this, so as to keep him. In a sense she had seduced herself. For the first time in her life she had accepted as a fact that she could end the day in bed with a man. 'Come, sit on my knee.' Tumble put his coffee on the floor and extended a paternal hand towards her. In the room there was a faint memory of his tobacco, a strong rich smell which reminded her of her father. She walked towards him, stopping in front of his chair. Why not this man? He had been kind to her, had looked after her. Why not any man?

Tumble grasped the back of her right leg with his left hand. He left it there for some time, long after she had stopped shivering with disgust at the feel of his moist palm sweating on her stocking. Neither Tumble nor Christine knew what to do next. They were saved further embarrassment by the timely intervention of the gas fire which chose this moment to run out of fuel. Tumble recognized this event by the sudden cooling of his ankles, which he promptly withdrew under his chair to retain the warmth they had absorbed earlier. Christine removed her leg from his clutch to go to the mantelpiece where she kept the shillings for the meter. While she was occupied with the shilling Tumble, with that sense of improvisation which had so far been confined to his lectures, got up from his chair to turn off the light. This made his task much easier: in the dark his clumsiness would be well disguised.

They met in the middle of the room, with only the light from the gas fire to help Tumble undo her clothes. While he was busy with the zips and the buttons she watched the shadows of his movements on the wall behind him. This was how she had imagined sex to be: mysterious, bizarre, a pantomime with no purpose.

When they were ready Tumble led her across to the bed where he went about his work clinically, with no emotion, but with a care for detail and craftsmanship. In spite of this she was tortured by the shock of his madness upon her, realizing too late the full force of her involvement in this alien primeval dance. When he finished she covered herself with a blanket and lay weeping for some time, caught up in the anguish of release.

Tumble dressed by the fire, pleased with his success. He was not surprised by the weeping. Such a reaction to the loss of virginity was normal enough in English women, especially when they had strong religious backgrounds. In other societies, where Judao-Christian thought had not been able to surround it with taboos, virginity was not nearly so sacred and its loss was a natural part of growing up. Western women were much too neurotic about the whole business of sex and motherhood. So much for the advantages of civilization.

An outburst of uninhibited sobs and tears from Christine interrupted his scholarly evasion of personal responsibility. The drama of the day had overpowered her at last. When Tumble came over to the bed, presuming to comfort her, she turned away from him. Having destroyed her, there was nothing he could do for her now.

'Go away,' she sobbed, her face to the wall. 'Please. Go home.'

'Time we went home,' Joachim said to Gerry as they finished the sixth or seventh glass of beer at their table in the corner of the common room. The pop group was packing the pop group equipment into pop group equipment bags, helped by two or three teenage girls who were not students but who had been allowed into the party because they had told the porter that they had come with the group. Now, having shared the group with strangers for a whole evening, they had their reward. They were going home with them.

Hollow music from a gramophone behind Nick Hill's bar reached the few couples still embracing and sweating on low couches near the walls. The ghosts from the light projector danced out of step over the walls and over their bodies catching them in surrealistic colours and poses. Their rites, so clothed, were rendered exotic and deceptively beautiful.

'You are right. This party has run its course. Now that the

wine has reached the dregs let us go before the vomiting begins.' Gerry was very drunk, so drunk in fact that his speech was now confusing himself as much as Joachim. He staggered to his feet too quickly so that he had to grab at the table in front of him to stop himself from falling face downwards on to it. Some empty glasses rolled on to the floor and across the empty room, travelling in boomerang half circles until they were stopped by a chair or a foot or by their own sense of the stupidity of proceeding further. One tumbler was not empty. It dropped like a bomb on to the hard floor where it exploded, scattering beer and sharp pieces of glass over the wall.

Joachim was more careful when he got to his feet. He took Gerry by the arm, lifting him off the table and back on to his feet very easily. It was the first time he had considered the possibility that he and Gerry might be drunk. 'Thank you, Joachim. I was not aware of the extent of my intoxication. I shall, as the policeman says, proceed with caution.'

They walked to the door, ignoring the mess of beer and glass on the floor beside their seats. None of the petting couples thought it worthwhile to interrupt their play to watch them. At the door they passed Nick Hill who was amusing two girls, who should have known better. With extreme abandon, in full view of anyone who might come into the room Nick Hill was sitting at a table by the door rolling reefers. All his equipment lay on the table, ready for inspection by anyone who thought himself an expert. Joachim and Gerry paused at the door, watching him, their own clumsiness emphasized by the meticulous craftsmanship.

In a small leather wallet, carefully wrapped in silver foil, he kept his thin wafers of marijuana, purchased from his contact at the current market price of seven pounds an ounce. From this wallet, now carelessly open at the side of the table he had taken a tiny square which he was now separating into fine strands on a piece of notepaper in front of him. While he was busy with the penknife he explained to the girls exactly what he was doing, why he was doing it and what he would do next. It was important to maintain the exact proportion of tobacco and pot, important to see that the distribution throughout the reefer was such that no marijuana was wasted. His hands worked all the time, separating, then mixing, then rolling. It was some time before the mixture was ready, some time before he was able to begin packing the cigarette paper. When he finished he held it up before him, explaining again why it was so long, why he had taken so much care with the filter, why it was necessary to taper the reefer so sharply at the other end. Then he stopped talking to light the work of art, feeling his way round the point with the flame of a match. He puffed it twice, before offering it to one of the girls. She must hold her breath, take the smoke down into her stomach and hold it. That way she would benefit.

Joachim and Gerry looked at each other in admiration. In everything this man did he was a technologist. He was twentieth-century man incarnate. As spokesman for them both Joachim felt something should be said, some tribute paid to the performance they had been privileged to see.

'Nick Hill,' he said, 'Technologist and Hedonist we salute thee.' They both bowed.

'Go in peace,' said Nick. So they did, taking with them two bottles of his Irish whiskey, which they kept secret from him. As he had probably pinched it from a man at the docks he could hardly complain if someone pinched it from him.

They left the building together, careful not to let the impatient porter see the extent of their drunkenness. They stepped out of the door into a shower which soaked their outer clothing before they could cross the road.

It was some time before they yielded to the mischief in the storm, a storm which had driven all living things indoors. The rain was coming down so fast that the drains and the gutters overflowed, covering road and pavements with a thin slippery veil which caught the crazy shapes of the tall street lamps and sent their reflections dancing into the windscreens of the few slow cars which had not yet reached home. Joachim and Gerry walked bravely to the corner of the square, looking the storm in the face and laughing at it. But the storm prevailed, forcing them to button their overcoats and then to hide in them, its massive purpose penetrating even their drunken foolishness.

At the corner of the square they met the wind, now mad with frustration. All day it had buffeted the city and its people. Since morning it had tested its strength against the tall buildings, battering their windows in its fury, unable to destroy its enemies, merely finding it possible to dislodge certain roof-tiles on old buildings which was not much of an achievement for one with so much ambition.

The wind and the rain were too much for Gerry. At the corner of the square, when Joachim was about to turn into the teeth of the wind, Gerry surrendered. His flat was near by. He would visit Joachim another night and they would consume the whiskey in more comfort. He waved to Joachim before he turned away.

The young men separated, turned their backs to each other, and walked away. Joachim had to walk into the needles of rain which stung his face, bringing the blood to his cheeks. He tried to cover himself with the collar of his overcoat but the water ran down his neck, under his shirt and across his chest. It was cold water, with no comfort in it. Its purpose was to humiliate, to remind him that he stood single against the physical world and that the physical world, if it chose, could destroy him.

He encountered many floods and pools on his way home, many sudden cascades and fountains, as drainpipes and guttering crumbled and fell away. He did not try to avoid them. When he was drunk his body could never accomplish that which his brain directed. When he was drunk his mind outpaced his body so that he was content to let it drift and wander, marvelling at the dichotomy.

Tonight he was thinking about storms, thinking about their power and their beauty, thinking about how they had been used in great works of literature by men who understood their mysteries. In the middle of a great storm King Lear had gone mad. This was not at all surprising: storms have such a lot to say on the subject of the human condition.

He arrived at the house before he realized where he was. He was so busy with his meditation on storms that he almost walked on to the next street. He turned up the steps and ran inside the front door which was open.

He stood inside the porch for a while, still amusing himself with his thoughts on storms and tempests, looking out at the rain which could no longer reach him. The water dripped from his coat on to the floor and on to his shoes, which were already wet through.

Looking down he saw the brown envelope from the pools firm, floating in a pool of water in the corner, its directive to post early for Christmas still legible. The envelope had been there when he had gone out that evening.

Eventually he grew tired of looking at the rain and he went inside. Had he not been so drunk he might have wondered why all the lights in the house were burning, why all the doors in the hall were open to the elements. It was not until he closed the front door and vestibule door, not until after he saw that the linoleum in the hall was wet and stained, that he began to suspect that all was not well in the house.

His first thought was to look for Vicky; perhaps she had gone out for cigarettes to the machine at the end of the road. She sometimes went out for cigarettes at this time, though lately she had taken to sending him out for them for her, saying that it was no time for a girl to be out on her own. But she couldn't have gone out tonight. Not in this weather surely.

She was not in her living-room. He looked in through the open door. The light was on, the fire low but there was no sign of Vicky; only some indication that she had been in there and that she had not long gone out. He went into her kitchen and there too he found the light on. But she was not there.

He paused outside her bedroom door, which like all the other doors on the ground floor, was open. He knocked and waited.

'Vicky,' he called out, 'are you in there?' But there was no reply.

He pushed the door open farther. He did not want to go into the bedroom in case he found Vicky entertaining a client; someone whose needs were so urgent that they had not had time to close the door. But there was no sound of any movement in the room, no conversation, nothing. Carefully, ready to retreat at the first sign of a hostile reception, he crept round the door.

Vicky lay on the bed. Her head had been smashed open, possibly by the small axe which lay beside it. Blood and brains spilled out over the pillow, coagulating sometimes in folds of the sheets and blankets.

Her body was covered in cuts and bruises; sharp, deep gashes ran in crazy rivers over her legs and arms, each one the result of a blow with the self-same axe.

It was an untidy and horrible death, so horrible that Joachim could not understand what he was seeing. When he did understand he was violently sick.

Sacrifice

I

Night was the best time to come. Dark night when the children were asleep and there were few people to disturb, no one in the empty streets hurrying, shivering, cursing the weather. Night was the best time to take the country by surprise, to invade the cities while people slept, to present them, in the morning, with the reality of the invasion.

So, while the people slept, it came, working its way over the face of the land, falling softly and indolently on houses and fields. The sudden chill in many bedrooms drew husbands and wives closer together as it threatened to remove what little warmth had been created in their beds. There was much hiding under blankets, many an indiscreet renewal of the comfort of electric blankets, some inarticulate grumbling at the ineffectiveness of certain forms of central heating.

Lorry-drivers noticed it first, they saw it coming to meet them, as they guided their rumbling giants along the empty roads at speeds in excess of the regulations. Soft splashes of water on the windscreen, easily removed by the rubber blades. Millions of white flakes falling on the road in front, disappearing into nothing on the surface of the black highway. Thirty miles on, the land was covered in a thin veil, the veil that fell from the sky in millions of silken flakes. Thirty miles on, visibility was low, too low for driving. All over the country, at approximately the same hour, lorry-drivers surrendered to the power of the snow. They took refuge in the greasy comfort of transport cafés, passing the rest of the night with chips, pintables and unpleasant reports of weather conditions in all the places they had hoped to travel. The women who waited for them had to postpone their pleasure until another time, while the prostitutes who served them in lay-bys and outside the transport cafés had to go back home and look to their mail order catalogues to pay the week's rent.

Lorry-drivers, policemen, postmen collecting mailbags at railway stations, engine-drivers. Human owls, who worked in the dark and slept when the sun was high, saw the snow come. They watched it settle, watched while it worked, like them, all night to prepare the world for the following day. They saw that it was patient, they admired its perseverance when the first flakes dissolved on the damp pavements and the work of foundation had to be done again. They recognized its strength, the power it had to visit them and interrupt their business, its arrogance in ignoring them while it went about its work.

There was wisdom in arriving in the night. Visitors asked to stay the weekend must behave carefully if they intend to stay for six months. They are advised to be subtle in their dealings with their host, to avoid, as far as possible, any points of conflict other than the irritation unavoidably created by their presence in his house.

By morning the snow had unmistakably arrived. It lay over the country, having reshaped the contours of its landscape during the dark hours. When the sun came up there was, for some glorious minutes, a period of brilliant discovery with the light finding new shapes, new reflections, sudden joy. There were no shadows, no sharp features on the horizon. Roofs, streets, fields and hedges wore the same thick coat, creating an impression of universal gentleness and peace. From above, the land looked like a pillow, newly-laundered.

There were disturbances as people awoke and prepared themselves for work; frantic activity with long shovels as sensitive husbands cleared suburban paths before kissing their wives in their suburban porches. Children leaving for school early, their heads full of new games and new ways of hurting each other. There were, too, the impotent gestures of regional administrators who sent out lorries loaded with sand and salt to clear the roads. The morning was full of queues at bus-stops, queues of cars and buses running late, the cancellation of train services. Shoe shops were asked for gumboots and galoshes, chandlers for paraffin and coalmen for more coal. No one could go anywhere very quickly and much of the nation's work was left undone. The conscientious set off for work early, taking their slow turn in the bus queues, complaining about the government while the passing cars sprayed dirty snow over their overcoats and trousers. Students, in general, stayed in bed, knowing full well that it was pointless to try to get to their establishments of education because none of their educators would turn up. In the afternoon the snow began to fall again, much to the annoyance of the men on the snow-clearing lorries who were forced to start again with their dispensation of salt and sand. Office workers left the offices early so as to arrive home in time for tea. There was much confusion over transport, opportunities for pompous officials to eject third-class passengers from first-class compartments, and further cancellation of train services. Those conscientious men and women, who had gone to work, suddeny found that it was time to go home, time to interrupt their conversations about the weather. Teachers at evening classes set about cancelling lectures in liberal studies.

The snow, having been expected at Christmas, had arrived at the end of January, catching the people unawares. 'Snow will fall on high ground and may spread southwards from Scotland during the afternoon.' The forecast had been a month early. Over Christmas it had rained. The snow had no scientific right to be here. It contradicted that complicated system of prediction which weathermen had been refining for years.

By evening the snow was thick again on the ground. Those paths which had been hurriedly cleared by daybreak were now white again, white and slippery. Piles of dirty snow hugged the sides of the main roads, refusing to melt away and run down the gutters into the drains. Long-distance lorry-drivers left their wives to report at their places of employment, fully expecting that they would be sent home at once to spend the night smoking or playing cards because they had slept all day and there was no sleep left in them. They saw that conditions were worse than they had been the previous night when they had been forced to shelter in their cafés.

In Westmorland five sheep, being stupid, walked into a deep ditch and died.

The following morning the nation woke up to the fact that the snow was a reality, that it was likely to be with them for some time and that they had better cope with it if they intended to carry on with the games and rituals which had occupied them before it had arrived. The show had to go on.

Christine lay shivering in Tumble's bed. It was much too cold to get up, much too cold to wander around the huge flat. Since the departure of his wife Tumble had spent little time in his flat. His promise to buy himself a gas fire was repeated every time the weather changed and promptly forgotten as soon as he turned on the heater in his car. His bed was warmer now that Christine had come to live with him but the living-room remained as it had always been: cold, ascetic, and as draughty as a church hall. There was no incentive to get out of bed, no advantage to be gained by leaving the warm blankets.

She reached out for the cigarettes which lay on a table at the side of the bed. When she had presented herself uninvited at Tumble's flat, with a suitcase in each hand, she had been so distraught, so near to breakdown that Tumble had tried every technique he knew to calm her down. He had given her whisky liberally diluted with hot water and he had produced a packet of very mild cigarettes with filter tips. Her prejudice against smoking, he told her, was foolish. Smoking would soothe her; it could be the saving of her sanity.

The first one had made her dizzy but the sensation was not unpleasant especially when it distracted her mind from wandering through other fields. Now, after smoking for ten days, she no longer felt dizzy when she filled her lungs with the blue vapours. But smoking did give her something to do, something to occupy her hands and lips while she pondered pessimistically on the probable events of the day.

She picked up the packet of cigarettes, took one out and placed her dry lips round the virgin filter. She put the packet back on the table, holding the cigarette in her mouth for an age before reaching out again for the matches.

Mrs Richards had been pretty decent really. She hadn't kicked her out. It had been more along the lines of a maternal chat, more in terms of an attempt to educate Christine to the dangers of entertaining wolves disguised as sheep. She was sure nothing had happened. Christine was such a good girl, quite the best tenant she had ever had, polite, tidy, and well brought up. She felt it her duty, because Christine was such a good girl, more like a daughter than a tenant, she felt she ought to warn her against putting too much trust in men. University lecturers were, if anything, worse than students or boy-friends. University lecturers were clever, very capable of turning an innocent girl's head if they wanted to. Some of them led very strange lives. If the play she had seen on the television was anything to go by then none of them had any respect for their marriage vows, out with a different woman every night of the week and their wives were as bad. No, Christine would be well advised to keep clear of university lecturers. Not that she would ever do anything like that, not for a moment did she think she would behave like those girls on the television, but it was better to be safe than sorry, better to be able to recognize the enemy in all his shapes and forms.

She was not going to get worked up about the man being in Christine's room after eleven o'clock because it was the first time it had happened and she was sure Christine would never do it again. In any case the evening had obviously been a special occasion. She had noticed that Christine was wearing a new dress, that she had been in all afternoon getting herself ready. Was it a party at the university or a dance perhaps? It didn't matter, it was none of her business and she was not one to pry into other people's affairs. What about another cup of tea?

Christine decided to light the cigarette. She took a match from the box and scraped it along the sandpaper edge. Yes, Mrs Richards had been very friendly about it all. All the time she was talking Christine had felt dirty and dishonest. In fact the whole conversation had been rather pharisaic. Thank God you are not as other tenants, Christine. Thank God you pay me your tithes regularly, in the manner laid down. Thank God I could rest in my bed knowing that you were entertaining a university lecturer in your room after closing time, knowing that, whatever happened, you would not turn our little temple into a disorderly house, that my honour would be safeguarded. Mrs Richards had been so sure of her virtue that she had almost told her, had almost confessed that no honour had been guarded, that, in fact, all honour had disappeared, that she had been guilty of drunkenness and debauchery, that her whole day had been spent in preparation for the gratification of lusty carnal appetites. With any other tenant, apparently, Mrs Richards would have taken this for granted.

She had been very upset when Christine had told her that she was moving. Couldn't understand how Christine could possibly be happy in another flat when in this one she had everything she needed, when she was almost as well off as she could be in her own home. White lies had not been enough to convince her. Christine had to invent a whopper about a friend suddenly struck down with a broken leg who needed her to look after her. Mrs Richards had felt betrayed, all those cups of tea gone to waste, whatever she had expected from Christine was not to be given her. Christine wondered, at the time, whether she ought to tell Mrs Richards the truth. Tell her that she was going to see that university lecturer and to tell him that she intended to live with him because she thought she was probably pregnant and she didn't know what to do. This would have made it easier for Mrs Richards. Once she had recovered from the shock of discovering that her trust in Christine had been betrayed she would be able to cope with Christine's departure in the appropriate manner. She would never forgive herself for thinking that some tenants could be more equal than others and she would enforce her rules of housekeeping with even more strictness than hitherto.

But, decent as Mrs Richards had been, she did not deserve the truth. In any case Christine was not so sure what the truth of the matter was. She was not so sure of anything any more.

It is not easy to smoke in bed without scattering ash over the sheets. Christine made up her mind to rush over to the switch of the electric fire and to rush back between the bankets while the room warmed. She succeeded in the first part of her plan but once she was out of bed she could not get back in. Once, she had risen early every morning with military precision, presenting herself refreshed and eager at the earliest of lectures when some of her colleagues stayed in bed or struggled in at the last moment with bleary eyes, unshaven chins and dirty necks. It was difficult to break the habit, even though her circumstances had changed so completely. She decided to dress: it would constitute a useful and salutary punishment for having stayed in bed so long.

Mrs Richards was no longer a problem. All that remained of that part of her life was the deceit practised at her departure. There were other problems now, other people to deceive. Like her parents.

She had, of course, gone home for Christmas. Home, to continue playing the little girl with her father. But this time the game had not been so easy. No longer innocent, she had found it difficult to ape the childishness of her former self. There was disbelief in the enthusiasm with which she had greeted her father as he met her at the station, synthetic mischief in her giggling during the Chinese meal they had eaten before he left her to go back to the office. Her father did not notice any change. As far as he was concerned this was his little girl, his own special plaything with whom he had enjoyed a relationship more pure and satisfying than with anyone he had ever known. She was the joy of his life, someone who possessed all those qualities he considered admirable in little girls. She was pretty and charming, able to tease or to please as the spirit moved her. Her life seemed to be governed by a spirit of fickle feminine components which left him gasping with delight at the myriad changes of personality and beauty which came over her in a single day. This was his beloved on whom he had bestowed all that he possessed, sparing neither patience nor money on her education, filling her life with every artifact which had been designed to bring joy to the heart of little girls. He had revealed to her the wonders of Covent Garden and the Sadler's Wells Ballet, the National Gallery, the Tower of London, and the funfair at Battersea. Her mind had been disciplined by the Sisters of the Christian Schools, broadened by annual visits to camping-sites in Southern Europe, filled with wonder at the stories and games he had invented for them to play. From the moment of her birth she had delighted him. She would continue to do so until he died. Her father did not notice any change.

The electric fire was warm now. Two parallel bars glowed dull red sending dead dry heat to circle her ankles. She dressed in front of it, taking her clothes from a chair by the mantelpiece and warming them in front of the bars before she put them on. It was a slow process, full of sloth and self-indulgence

but she was in no hurry and self-indulgence was all she had
now.

Her mother had taken her moments of indiscreet seriousness
for maturity, commenting, when she caught Christine gazing
out of the window when she should have been stealing the hot
mince pies, that we all must grow up and wasn't it sad.

She had got through the holiday without breaking down,
without revealing to her parents that this Christmas was different from all the others. They had made it easier for her. When
her mother had told her not to pull the crackers before dinner
then she knew that she must pull the crackers before dinner or
they would think that all was not well. But there had been
times when she could have crawled into a hole and died. During Midnight Mass, for instance, when they all sang Silent
Night after the Communion, she had felt rotten inside, as if
there was a tumour as big as a football and as hungry as a swarm
of locusts, lusting and gorging on what was left of her self-
respect. She could not go to Communion. She could not take
God into her mouth when her soul was festering and decom-
posing, stinking with a fierceness infinitely more destructive
than a battlefield of corpses, than a drinking fountain full and
overflowing with typhoid fever. Her family went together to
the altar rails leaving her behind in the pew. She lied to her
mother. Told her that her stomach was upset and that she did
not want to receive the Host and then vomit, a lie which must
have offended God more than anything she had ever done.

She put on an extra sweater before she reached down and
turned off the electric fire. In the kitchen she could turn on all
the rings on the gas cooker while she was waiting for the water
to boil. She did not wash; it was much too cold and, in any
case, she wasn't going anywhere.

Tumble had gone to the university. He had said something
about snow before he had left but in his present mood, nothing
short of an earthquake or a nuclear explosion could keep him

out of the department of Sociology and Social Administration. She had heard him start his car, had tried to sleep through the barking and coughing of the engine as it laboured and skidded on the drive. But she hadn't paid much attention. Since she had come to live with Tumble she had discovered that it was sensible to ignore him most of the time. He lived in a world of his own, rarely saw things which bawled and shouted under his nose. He was a kind enough man but his kindness lacked sympathy. His kindness was a form of politeness, an etiquette which he had learned. It was not real kindness but playing at being kind. There was no emotion in the man at all.

His head was full of generalizations and predictions. When Christine had descended upon him that evening he had nodded wisely as she related her sad story. He understood, he had assured her. But what he had understood was not how she was suffering, or what she felt like to have to insist that he take some responsibility for the state she was in. What he understood was how she fitted into his statistical order of things. He knew the returns of the Registrar General on the incidence of illegitimacy, of abortion and of suicide, for every year since the war. His enthusiasm for her cause had its origins of his excitement at becoming involved with a statistic, with an example of deviant behaviour. His academic discipline had pretensions to scientific logic and scientific detachment. It seemed that Tumble, in seeking to eliminate bias from his research, had himself become objective, divorced utterly from any emotional involvement with the human condition. This was his problem: he had become the Compleat Sociologist and his intimate conversations were as human as articles in the *American Journal of Sociology*.

Christine had given up trying to talk to him. When he came home from the university they exchanged greetings and the symptoms of a conversation could be distinguished as the evenings progressed. But there was no meaning in these conversations; no real communication. It was as if Tumble could not distinguish between one person and another, modifying his behaviour only in terms of the differing social situations in which he found himself. To bus-conductors or barmen he might be patronizing, to women, polite and charming. It seemed that he played at being human. When he spoke he stood back to watch the words and sentences struggle towards the other person, unaware that they floundered and drowned in the swamp which he had placed between himself and everyone outside him.

Christine was not sure what to make of him. He played a curious role, a compound of Don Juan, Knight, and father. It was difficult to isolate which of these parts appealed to him most as he made no distinction between them, not even in his relationship with her.

The rings on the gas cooker lit themselves as soon as she turned the knobs above the oven. The kitchen was small, with a door which closed itself to comply with the fire regulations. There was a sink made of stainless steel, cupboards built into the wall for delft, small containers arranged in a neat line beneath a box of shelves suspended on the wall opposite the cooker. Under the window there was a small refrigerator in which the tenant could keep her frozen peas. In a corner near the fridge was a collection of flower-pots of varying shapes and sizes. One huge pot was separate from the others; it stood right in the corner, scrubbed and shining, waiting for whatever destiny Tumble had determined for it. He had asked Christine not to move it, had made a point of indicating something special was in store for this pot. Perhaps a palm or a rubber plant which he had dreamed up in his vision of himself as an Interior Decorator.

Sometimes Christine used this pot as a waste bin, filling it with household refuse, but she had nothing to throw away this morning. Instead, she filled the electric kettle at the sink by the window. It was here that she first saw the snow, here, while she

N

was filling the kettle that she looked out of the window and saw the miserable birds huddled on the branches of the trees in the garden, looking down at the thick snow which was keeping them from their breakfast. Later she would throw them some bread; there was no reason why every living thing should suffer simply because she had been foolish.

Joachim's mouse had disappeared. It might have been driven away by the smell of death which had hung in the house for so long. It might have had its peace of mind disturbed by the many comings and goings of policemen and pressmen with their pryings and probings for facts, clues, circumstantial evidence and human angles. Or it may have died, along with the rest of the house.

Joachim was the only living thing left. The sounds of life and movement in the house were his sounds, his movement. His room was the last remaining pocket of oxygen, an air bubble trapped in a pool of black pitch. Life had fled the other rooms, running out down the stairs and through the front door, leaving behind no ghosts or shadows, no light, nothing. Isolated lumps of furniture froze in a moment, never to move or breathe again until the life returned. Inanimate things, no longer because objects are related to subjects by verbs which are words of action and life. Here there was no action, here there was no possibility of the relation of one thing to another. There were only artifacts, things which had once been made, now separated from that force which had been responsible for their having come to be.

Light burned and flickered in Joachim's room but it was like the dying screams of the last votive lamp in a church at night. In this feeble, fickle glow Joachim lived a vegetable life, while the horror and the hell stormed his sanctuary from all sides.

At first he had been angry. At first he had cursed Vicky's murderer and his unnecessary violence, his soul tormented with the stupidity and cruelty of man in his moments of madness. He had wept in anger. The policemen had found him weeping as he caressed Vicky with fine soap and soft towel, trying to restore some human dignity to what was left of her body. They had mistaken his sorrow for contrition. They had handled him roughly, snatching him away from the bloodstained bed, bundling his towel and soap into polythene envelopes, along with the axe and some samples of blood and hair.

In the police station they had accused him of murder and it was then that his anger broke. In one lightning second of eternity he had transcended the human condition: words and phrases fell from his lips in storms and earthquakes. There was such beauty in his language, so many different emotions and images, that the police station became, for the duration of his catharsis, a holy place, an oracle where men should walk barefoot.

He would never remember what he had said then, nor how long it had taken him to say it. But he would always remember that sense of release which was with him when it was over. Virtue had gone out of him, as it had gone out of Christ when the woman touched his cloak. He would never be able to describe that experience. It had been a time when his soul had dominated his body, when what he said was not produced by his reason or his prejudice or his pain. What he said found its inspiration and its forms of expression somewhere within him, some part of him which had not made itself known to him before but which had chosen that moment in time to take over.

The policemen, convinced that he had not murdered Vicky, later charged him with obstructing them in the course of their duty. He had no legal right, they said, to mess about with the body before they arrived.

His visitors from the Press had not impressed him. As soon as news of the murder spread he had to open his door to sensation hungry reporters and photographers who visited him, day and night, to bully him into making statements which they could scribble into their shorthand notebooks and use in evidence against him later. It was not long before he grew tired of the newspapermen, not long before he ignored their repeated hammerings at his door. They reacted by making up facts about him – they had to have a story and if he was not going to supply them with the truth then he could hardly complain if they printed lies. His photograph appeared alongside photographs of Jenny Oak and Vicky, so that the British public might spot him easily when he walked down the street.

Someone told the Press that Vicky had been a prostitute and, as far as the readers could make out, this made Joachim a pimp and Jenny Oak a keeper of a brothel.

One morning he had been provoked enough to pour opprobrium on the heads of the Press from his window overlooking the front door. This was a foolish act. He was photographed doing it and the pictures were published in the evening newspapers with headlines and captions which tried to make out that he lived an Elizabethan life and that his standards of hygiene were of those times. The bucket he had emptied on the reporters had contained cold clean water but the newspapers hinted that its contents were more sensational, misrepresentations which were believed by the municipal health authorities and by Joachim's stepmother, so that two letters arrived from these two public consciences, warning Joachim of impending visits.

By now the reporters had gone. The police had found their man eventually. He was a small respectable librarian with glasses and a little wife and home out in the suburbs. Joachim did not know how the police had tracked him down but they were working on the theory that he had one hell of a kink about religion and sex. Perhaps his name had come out of their files. Perhaps he had a habit of dressing up as a nun in his spare time, like some of those nuts who turn up at the scenes of mining disasters and floods. Joachim had never seen him in the house before. As far as he knew, he was not one of Vicky's regular clients.

By the time the reporters found out about him the police had the librarian charged and the case *sub judice* so that they had to wait until the judgement before they could really go to town on his private life. In the meantime they had their livings to earn so they had all disappeared from Joachim's house to get in some other victim's hair.

The house was very still when he went down for the mail. He always found the mornings frightening. There was no sound of children playing and fighting in the basement: Bonnie Prosper had found the publicity attendant on the murder bad for business. She had moved out, taking her illegal kindergarten with her. Joachim had not seen her go. She had waited till the early hours of the morning so that she could avoid the Pressmen. A car had picked her up at the end of the street and whisked her off out of his acquaintance.

There were two letters in the porch. One was for Gordon. Odd that Gordon should have friends naïve enough to believe that he could still be living in this house, that he could have escaped the ravages of the police and the publicity. Gordon had been taken away to a mental hospital. The university authorities had thought it best, under the circumstances, to send two porters and half a dozen unfeeling medical students to carry him off. This scene pleased the Press but it embarrassed the university authorities, who had not expected the Press to be on hand.

The other letter was for him. It had a local postmark and had come from the university, a fact he was able to establish without opening it because the name of the university was printed on the envelope. It was not an official letter, being addressed in longhand. He opened it as he went back upstairs.

Dear Joachim,
    If, and when, you decide to come out of hibernation could

you let me have the piece about Alpha and Beta – I've promised it to a student for a satirical magazine he wants to produce. Don't expect it will have much of a circulation but I have reached the stage where I must see something of mine in print soon or I might go berserk.

Some news for you to keep you going. They are creating a third chair in the department and rumour has it that Tumble's arse is the only one big enough to fit. Pentup has not been seen since he went to investigate the activities of the Socialist Labour League three weeks ago. Warble is furious about the O.B.E. Says it must have resulted from a clerical error in the lower offices of the Home Office. Seems to be writing a vicious attack on the honours system in revenge.

If you feel up to it drop into the department soon and we'll have some of that whisky.

Gerry.

Warble's O.B.E. had been the funniest item in the New Year's Honours List. He had expected a knighthood at least. O.B.E.s are not given to professors. They are for pop singers and rural postmen, for social workers, provincial trade union officials and professional footballers. To offer a professor an O.B.E. is to insult him. No wonder Warble was upset.

Joachim put on the kettle for coffee. The kitchen window looked out on to the backyard and the garage where Vicky's car lived while the police decided what to do with it. There were other backyards beyond the garage. The walls stuck out like pieces of fruit cake iced with a thick layer of snow.

The Alpha-Beta piece must be in that envelope Gerry had given him in the pub the night Vicky was murdered. He hadn't read it yet but if it was satire he would look at it while he drank his coffee because satire was how he felt. Nasty, vicious and unsentimental, bitter with the disillusionment of failing to live with principles in a world which was materialist to the core.

That is how he felt: alone, unloved, and unappreciated, a victim of his own and other people's mistakes.

The kettle boiled, interrupting his narcissistic suffering. Soulfully he made the coffee. Miserably he went into the bedroom to pause in front of the mirror and contemplate his persecuted image before he collected Gerry's envelope from the pocket of his jacket. Bravely he opened it and took it over to his chair to read it and grapple with the problems it posed.

A FURRY TAIL

Once, in a far-off culture, there were two sociologists, and they lived in a small house in the middle of a large field. The field, and the house, and indeed the whole culture, had been conquered by the great ogre Science and everyone who lived there had to work for him.

Everyone was afraid of the ogre Science. He had conquered the culture in a pitched battle with the Prince Religion who had ruled over the culture before him. The people had been happy with the Prince Religion as their ruler; they had spent their days in dreaming of heaven and in gathering flowers for the many pretty shrines which the Prince Religion had built for them. Under this new master dreaming was forbidden and everyone had to work. And there was no place for them to go to when they died.

The two sociologists had to work very hard to please the ogre Science. He had been to visit them once, just after he had become their master, and he had warned them that if they did not do what they were told, he would take away their house and their field and give them to someone else. The sociologists were afraid of the ogre Science. He had changed their names. In future they were to be called Alpha and Beta, because that was a scientific way of putting it. When he announced this, the ogre had stood outside the door of the small house and laughed and laughed until the small house trembled in the field, and the one great eye of the ugly giant wept and became bloodshot. The ogre had gone away from the small house but he had warned the two sociologists that he would send his Chief Inspector once a month to examine their work. The two sociologists lived in fear of the ogre Science, and of the monthly visit of the Chief Inspector.

Every day they had to go out into the field and gather data. The field was full of data and every evening when they went back into the house their sacks were full and their arms tired with carrying them. Some data were large and some were small, and the data was made up of every colour of the rainbow. When they had finished gathering data, they would carry their sacks into the house and leave them by the door while they sat down to their mug of beer and their bread and cheese.

Later in the evening they would pick up their sacks and carry them to separate corners of the room, where they would sit down and empty the sacks on to the floor. The ogre Science had given them some machines to help them in their work and Alpha always used these machines. But Beta did not like them. Noisy, smelly things he called them, and he did not like them. One of the machines was called a Statistic, and Alpha was very fond of this machine. Every night, as soon as he had finished his beer and cheese, he would rush over to his sack and empty it into the machine which would champ and gurgle very contentedly as he turned the handle.

When all the data had been fed into the machine Statistic, and when the machine had done all it could for the data, Alpha would take the results over to his workbench. He would stand there for a long time. Sometimes he would say

'That is significant', and he would smile, and sometimes he would say 'That is not significant at all', and he would look rather sad.

Whenever he said 'That is significant' he would collect his significant data together and take it to the table where he was building a model for the ogre Science. He built a small model every evening, but he was also building a very big one which he said would explain everything. The ogre Science would be pleased when he saw the big model; it is very scientific. The small models were scientific also but they were very small and did not explain everything. He had lots of little models and he called them by different names. One was called 'Role set', and another 'Communication system in small work group', but they were only little models and anyone could make them. His large model was called 'Society', and it explained everything. Alpha said that the ogre Science would be so pleased with it that he would give them a bigger house. Their own house would be too small to hold the model when it was finished. The spare bedroom was used up already.

Beta did not like using the machines and he did not like building models. While Alpha was working at the table muttering about causal and technological explanation and the hypothetico-deductive method, and occasionally shouting joyfully, 'I've found another continuum', Beta sat on the floor in the corner and arranged his data in pretty patterns in front of him. He loved the way he could mix the colours and shapes of the data and he would spend entire evenings amusing himself in this way.

Alpha would often warn him that he was not being scientific and that the ogre Science would be angry with him. But Beta did not care. He did not like working for the ogre Science. When the Prince Religion had ruled the culture, Beta had been the chief flower arranger at the national shrine, and he had been very happy. The ogre Science had made him into a sociologist because his 'A' levels made him unsuitable for anything else. But he did not like being a sociologist; he hated the machines and he hated models.

One evening Alpha came over to the corner of the room where Beta was playing with his data and examined the patterns on the floor. He looked at the patterns and he looked sadly at Beta, shaking his head all the while. Suddenly something significant struck him on the back of the neck and he said urgently:

'I see you are not using any yellow data.' Beta looked up at him and felt very guilty.

'I do not like yellow data,' he said quietly, 'it hurts my eyes.'

'But you can't simply leave out yellow data. Everything you do will be biased. Give me some,' said Alpha.

'I haven't got any,' replied Beta, looking even more guilty than before.

'Why haven't you got any? You must have some if you used your Random Sample Properly,' said Alpha.

'I threw it away,' said Beta, 'it was too heavy to carry through the fields.'

Alpha became very worried. Beta was worse than he thought. He paced up and down for a long time, and when it was time to go to bed, he did not say 'Goodnight' to Beta, but carried on pacing up and down, his brow furrowed and his head bent.

He did not go to bed at all that night. Beta could hear him banging and knocking with something all through the dark hours. In the morning, when Beta went into the room to see what Alpha was doing, he was very surprised. The room was full of wood shavings and bits of coloured glass, and Alpha was sitting in one of the chairs with a green shade over his eyes and a long stick in his hand. When he saw Beta he called out to him:

'I have solved your problem. You need not worry about yellow data hurting your eyes any more. If you wear this it will protect you. It is called an Inter Viewing Schedule and it will prevent the yellow data from hurting your eyes. The stick is called a Probe and it is for discovering yellow data which tries to hide behind other data. Put on the Inter Viewing Schedule and take the Probe and let us test them in the field.'

While Alpha and Beta were in the field, a dirty tramp knocked at the door of the small house. No one answered so he opened the door and went into the room. When he got inside and saw all the models and the machines, he clapped his hands with joy. He took a frying-pan from the kitchen and went from one model to another, selecting data here and there, and putting them into the pan. When the pan was full, none of the models could stand up because the tramp had taken away all the supporting data. When the pan was full, the tramp held it over the fire for some minutes, and when the data was cooked, he ate it.

He left the house before Alpha and Beta returned. He swung happily down the lane, his spirits high and his belly full. It was not every morning that breakfast came so easily.

Of course he had not used any yellow data. Being a tramp, his life depended on his ability to tell the difference between mushrooms and toadstools.

Joachim finished the piece and put it down. He was not quite sure what Gerry was getting at. There was some argument in there, hidden among the puns and the plays on words. What was it? Artist and Scientist possibly, losing out to real people because their perceptions were governed by false laws. Or was it simply an attack on sociologists so involved with their methods of investigation that they could no longer see the wood for the trees. Mushrooms and toadstools, what were they? The stuff of life perhaps, meaningful only to those who did not take them too seriously. He had liked the comment about religion.

A knock at his door saved him from further work. It was probably Jenny Oak who came to see him quite frequently now. She seemed grateful that he had not deserted her house after the crisis. She was more serious with him now: the murder had revealed her whole life to him through the pages of the newspapers. She did not have to play at being a woman with him any more. If they slept together now it was on more equal terms with no secrets hidden away in dark corners. She was probably bringing him some food. Bringing him food and sleeping with him was how she thanked him for his loyalty.

He opened the door to her, wondering where she would figure in Gerry's parable on the human condition. Mushroom, toadstool, or tramp?

Tumble was happy. He was happy enough to hum a merry Hebridean folk tune as he worked systematically through his filing cabinets. The creation of this new chair had been a bolt from the blue. With the government clamping down on every pound the universities were spending and with the other faculties in the university complaining so often about how over-staffed the department of Sociology and Social Administration was, and how little use it seemed to them to be to anyone or anybody, he could not understand how it had been allowed to happen. The Science faculties had always considered that two professors in the department were two too many. How on earth had they let this pass when they were so short of money themselves? A clerical error possibly, like the one responsible for Warble's O.B.E.

Still the Chair was there and he was the favourite to fill the post. Pretty was being rather kind about it all, saying that he would apply because he was expected to but that he would support Tumble's application because he thought Tumble was the right man for it and he wasn't. Good of him really because he might have stood a fair chance if he had put his mind down to it.

Putting one's mind to it was easier said than done. How simple it would be if it were a mere matter of filling in a form. But it wasn't. He had to present a detailed history of his career as a university teacher, with a list of his research projects and publications, his experience in industry and his knowledge of administration. He was also expected to include a list of offers he had received from other universities, giving the reasons why he had turned them down. Some offers were obviously more impressive than others. Should he mention that American university, for instance, which had asked him to become their professor of Speech? The committee might laugh their heads off.

The reasons I did not accept any of these offers are found mainly in my satisfaction with this university and my experience of it. I have been very happy here. My superiors have always allowed me the freedom to research into those aspects of behaviour which most interest me. The library is excellent and my colleagues charming and co-operative. I refused the chairs in the new universities because I did not believe in what was going on there. Here we have a healthy traditional streak in our organization of student courses which prevents us from offering such degrees as Bachelor of Science in Sociology and Market Gardening, which are available at these newer places of learning.

That should please the committee. Most of them did not like what was happening in the newer universities, mainly because the newer universities were attracting the better students with their four-year courses and mixed halls of residence. It was a silly idea anyway this interview. He knew the members of the committee very well and they knew him. All this ritual was like filling in an application form to ask a prospective father-in-law for his daughter's hand in marriage. The external assessor, called in by the university to make sure that they did not make a mistake in appointing the wrong man, was a professor in a chair which Tumble had rejected when it was offered to him.

He was certain to be appointed. But he had to go through the ritual of preparing his application. He didn't mind. It was fun really. He scattered papers all over his room. He had written so much and had published so much that it would be weeks before he had everything compiled and tabulated.

His door opened and a head peered round. It was the gaunt head of Charles Pretty, smiling.

'I didn't know you were so busy. I'll come back later if you like,' he said through the smile.

'No. Do come in, Charles. I'm only clearing out my files. Come in and sit down.'

Pretty slid into the room, still smiling. He sat down on the arm-chair near the radiator, spreading his arms over the warm pipes as a snake stretches out to sunbathe on the branch of a tree.

'It is rather a waste, don't you think? If one's own department is ignorant of one's important contributions in the fields of research and theory then one should not have to go through all this' – he lifted a hand from the radiator and cast it in an arc over Tumble's papers – 'don't you agree?'

'It is rather tiresome, Charles, but I must confess that I am enjoying it. I haven't seen some of this stuff for ages. One writes so much that one forgets certain items very easily.'

'Surely they won't want everything. Not every little article and essay.'

'Down to the last memo, Charles.' Tumble was so happy he could make little jokes. But then he had nothing else to do. 'And budget reports.'

'What is a budget report?' Charles made the phrase seem philistine and pornographic.

'At the bottom of the list of projects one must add a note indicating which of them made a profit. Profit, in this context, is a loose term. It includes the money left over after a project has been completed together with monies received from the sale of articles.'

Charles Pretty sank deeper into his chair, overcome by the bureaucracy of it all. He closed his eyes in suffering. Tumble, meanwhile, continued with his catalogue. Pretty always amused him. The man had a monastic respect for scholarship and he assumed that everyone shared his innocence. Even the youngest of the research assistants knew more about the game of political manœuvre than he did. He was too much of a philosopher and not enough of a sociologist: too many ideas and no facts. Talking to him was like telling a child about sex.

Charles Pretty opened his eyes as soon as he recovered. He watched Tumble playing with his papers, noticed the superior and confident smile tickling the lips, the eyebrow raised in self-worship. He gripped the radiator hard before he spoke.

'Quentin.' His tone was serious, demanding urgent attention.

'Yes.' Tumble was quick to respond, pausing in his work to look the man in the eye.

'What are you going to do about the girl?'

'Girl?'

'You know that the vice-chancellor is rather puritan about these things. I felt I ought to mention it because they could use it as an excuse not to give you the appointment. Perhaps if you were to marry her . . .' His voice disappeared down an embarrassed tunnel as it looked for somewhere to hide.

Tumble smiled again. How helpful of Charles to think of that. The poor man. If the committee did not want to give him the job they could use any excuse, any pretext. If they were going to give him the job they would give it to him, irrespective of Christine or of anything else he had done. They would regard him as charming or as immoral, depending on whether or not they had decided to give him the chair. Poor, innocent Charles, to think such things mattered.

'If they use that as an excuse then they will use anything. In any case, Charles, I don't think she would marry me. She's a strange girl. Roman Catholic, great sense of guilt, Electra complex, not the sort of relationship it seems from the outside.'

'I hope you're right.'

Charles Pretty uncurled his body from the chair and the radiator, rising to his feet slowly with the fluid, sinister motion of a cobra rising to the rhythm of a snake-charmer. He slipped a hand under his jacket at the point where his wallet met his chest.

'Is it true that your project has been cancelled? Rumour has it that Warble has diverted the grant to finance his essay on the State's maldistribution of public reward for heroic work.' Both laughed, quickly.

'True, Charles. I'm happy to be rid of it. I don't care for industrial sociology. No concepts of its own and no theory. All labour turnover and restriction of output. So boring.'

'What will you do with that research assistant?'

'Ryan? I expect Ryan will have to go. He can't grumble; he's had a year's salary for doing nothing.'

'When you get this chair you might be able to use him, as they say, in another capacity.' Charles Pretty smiled at his own sense of humour.

'I don't think so, Charles. I shall probably send him away with glowing references. He will get a job easily enough.'

'Perhaps I might find a use for him.'

'You are welcome to him, Charles. I'm afraid he and I have strained our professional relationship to its limits.'

Charles Pretty paused at the door. Since he had risen from his chair he had made steady progress to that part of the room.

'Are you saying that he knows too much about you?'

'In a way, yes.'

'Ah.'

'Are you going for coffee, Charles?'

'Yes. Will you join me?'

'I think so. I'm growing tired of this nonsense.' Tumble waved a modest hand over the pile of articles, offcuts, reprints, manuscripts and notes on his desk.

Pretty opened the door for Tumble as he went out of the room. They walked the corridor almost abreast, with Pretty an imperceptible six inches behind Tumble. As they approached the 'DOWN' staircase they missed the noise of the window banging in Tumble's room. It had opened in obedience to the vacuum created by Pretty when he closed the door. In Tumble's room a soft cleansing wind blew over his papers, pushing some of them off the desk into the waste paper basket and over the floor. Some lighter pieces were carried out of the window. They floated over the street like paper aeroplanes, settling on the heads of children and the roofs of cars. Some were driven into the gutters by the traffic, others were run over by buses.

2

Christine dreamed that it was last term again and she had done nothing wrong. Her world was solid, rock hard. She went to mass and came out feeling good, feeling that she belonged in the land of religion and the disciplined life. It was such a beautiful dream with everyone behaving as she thought they should and everything fitting into the pattern written in her strength. She was, naturally, the centre of the dream, the focal point of every interaction. People saw her and went away uplifted, threatened her and went away defeated, sought her help and found it in the disciplined advice she felt able to offer. She was strong with the immunity of multiple rules and regulations, the vaccinations of her childhood and her time at school. Her religion was, for herself and others, an ever present help in times of trouble and though she walked in the valley of death, no evil could approach her.

When she awoke she felt the pain of knowing that what had been was no more, that what had been real was not fantasy, that what was real now was a nightmare. If only she could reach out and touch something real. Something which would respond, comfort her, tell her in soft sweet words that nothing had really changed, that she had been ill and that now she would be better. She could not live without strength, without nourishing this strength in the wisdom of centuries of scholarship and learning. There was no strength in the things about her, no wisdom. There were things, solid things: wooden furniture, walls, a river and a garden. But these things were not part of her. She had not made them or bought them, or received them as gifts. They were there as part of the nightmare, to torment her. There was no nourishment in them, as there was no nourishment in Tumble.

There were no streams of Babylon where she could sit down

and weep, no respite from the multitudes of enemies who made war on her, at every turn.

There was life within her, she knew that now. But it was the life of the monster growing in her belly, the cancer of her sin swelling large until it burst. The child, conceived in sin, must have evil heaped upon it from its birth. There was no food for it in her, just as there was no food for her here. Its eucharist was her wickedness and it must feed upon her nightmare. Its germination had been the beginnings of her destruction; its birth must kill her, dead.

There was no shape to her life, just as there would soon be no shape to her body. And there was nothing, nothing at all, which she could do to change her destiny. From now on, every step she took would hurt someone. Herself mostly, and her parents, Tumble, because she would never marry him, Joachim, because she had betrayed him. And her God, because she refused to be forgiven.

'I feel yellow,' she had told Tumble at breakfast. Yellow, the colour of dead grass, of bruised apples, of skin under bandages, of broken eggs.

'That's pretty. Yellow is a good colour to feel.' Tumble was thinking of buttercups and children's toys.

She ought to get out more. Out into the sunlight. Perhaps, today, she would go down to the university. She could gossip about the Child Care course with those students who were still in regular attendance. She might meet Hazel and talk to her about nothing. Or would Joachim see her there. Would he recognize her despair and sweep her off over the river on the ferry boat. If Joachim had fathered her monster they could have married in church, with parents and candles, silver and gold, an acolyte swinging incense, their lives sprinkled with holy water.

'I think I may go down to the university today.'

'That's a good idea. You should get out more. Would you like to come down with me?'

'No, thank you. I don't want to go down there so early. I'll take a bus.'

To go with Tumble would be to commit herself to going. She was not sure that she would actually go down to the university. She had suggested it as an idea, as something she could think about to distract her from thinking about the nightmare. She might go, she might not. Making the decision would take time, would give her something to do.

Through the window she could see the sun burn feebly behind a grey cloud. The snow had begun to melt the day before but there was so much of it that it would be days before it had disappeared altogether. The lawn was coming back to the garden. There were damp green patches showing through the wet snow, the first of many signs that the temperature was lifting. There were birds in the garden again. During the siege she had fed them on breadcrumbs and bits of limp spaghetti which she thought they might mistake for worms. They could get along without her now.

She could see the river, swelling brown and mysterious, with the occasional hint of white horses. She thought it would be good to go down to the river this morning. She could walk there, along the private promenade, or lean on the painted rail, near the old boathouse.

She put on her duffel coat, leaving the breakfast dishes unwashed on the dining-table. She had given herself a long sensual, dilatory bath the previous evening so she assumed her face and hands were clean enough to pass any normal inspection without further treatment.

At the front gate it was left for the river and right for the bus-stop. She turned left, passing the notice which warned the public and stray dogs that they were in danger of prosecution if they were caught on the promenade.

She started her walk at the far end of the promenade, near the ugly docks which sometimes spat oil and grease on to the river. There was a high wall there, to keep out industrial spies, and it seemed as good a spot as any to begin her journey. There was a narrow paved footpath, separated from the road by a strip of green lawn, which was much cleaner than the lawn in the garden because the man in charge of the park had been to sweep away the snow.

She walked slowly, one hand in the pocket of her duffel coat, and the other bouncing on the iron rail put there to prevent her from falling in the river. It was a cold day. The sun had lost its battle with the clouds and there was a slight wind. It was not an unfriendly wind but it was mischievous enough to tickle the river into movement and then to·topple the tops of the waves into splashes of white foam. Above the river there were many seagulls, gliding and circling at different heights and then swooping down on to the water to seize some small thing which they had seen from the sky. Christine could not imagine what the river had to offer these birds. There could be nothing alive in those brown velvet wastes. What were the seagulls eating?

She stopped as soon as she reached the old boathouse. Her father had he been with her, would have told her stories of smugglers and pirates. At least he would have done in the old days. If he were with her now he would be out of his mind trying to adjust to the fact of his daughter's defilement. There were no pirates any more. Just the one monster who was very real.

The boathouse was set back from the river and was approached by a small narrow channel of dirty water. Flotsam rocked in the channel; bits and pieces of waste matter from the houses in the park, two long planks rubbing against a slimy wall. She stared into the channel for a long time, thinking how suitable a place for her to drown. One more load of human excrement, lost among the sewage and the contraceptives.

She turned her back on the river to walk back up the road past the flat to the bus-stop. She bought some chocolates in a newsagents and ate them with a kind of perverse satisfaction while she waited for the bus. She knew she didn't deserve them. The bus came sooner than it should have done and she was down at the university in fifteen minutes.

It was too cold to wander round the university buildings. She thought she might find someone in the students' common room in the department of Sociology and Social administration. She went in through the double doors, smiling out of habit at the porter as she went past him. Down the stairs, through the room with the table tennis table where the atmosphere was already foul with human sweat, and into the coffee room, where she was surprised to see all her colleagues from the Child Care course gathering as if in preparation for an expedition.

'Hello, Christine. How are you?' One of the older men came over to her when she went into the room.

'Hello, Arthur. I've not been well lately but I'm feeling much better now, thank you.' There was something of her former self in her reply.

'Jolly good. Are you coming with us?'

'Where are you going?'

'To the medical museum.'

'No thanks. I don't feel that well.'

'Rubbish. There's no harm in it. I'll get you a coffee before I try to persuade you.' Arthur went to the hole in the wall where the coffee was dispensed. He had no need to persuade Christine to go with them because their lecturer in Psychology had just come through the door.

'Good morning, Christine. Are you feeling better? I'm glad you could come for the visit to the medical museum. It's very important that you should see what they have. Not much point my preaching about heredity if you can't see some of the things which are inherited. Very useful for your examination too, I shouldn't wonder.'

'I'm quite well, thank you, Mr Flagg.' Christine answered his inquiry, undistracted by the homily which came after it. So the Child Care course were going to the medical museum to see something connected with heredity. What could that be? Diseases? Venereal diseases passed on to children at birth like Elizabeth I. Not much fun in that. Still, she could use it as a sort of punishment. Torment herself with the possibilities in store for her monster. She couldn't get out of it now anyway. The man Flagg had seen her. Part of the nightmare.

'Here's your coffee.' It was Arthur again. 'I see Flagg was talking to you. Did he convince you that you should come with us?'

'He made it impossible for me not to.' Christine took the coffee from him and smiled at him to thank him for bringing it over.

'Good. Then I need say no more except to welcome you back to the land of the living.'

'Thank you.'

'It looks as though Flagg is ready to leave. The others are gathering about him like imprinted ducks.'

'Like what?'

'Ducks. Imprinting. You know.'

'A psychological joke.' The lecture on learning theory had taken place before Christmas. Imprinting had been the first point discussed. It had been accompanied by photographs of maladjusted ducks running after an old man because they thought he was their mother. Everyone had laughed, which was why the lecture had been so easy to remember. When he moved they followed him, just like the ducks.

Christine attached herself to the tail of the line of students, following them out of the building and down the street to the Faculty of Medicine, which contained the medical museum. When they reached the building there was a man waiting for them at the door. He shook hands with Flagg and made a short, humorous speech to the students. Christine couldn't hear what he said because she was at the back of the line and there was too much noise from the buses going past. After the speech they went inside.

Everything in the medical building seemed to be made of marble. The floors were marble, there were marble pillars supporting a very high roof, and tablets recognizing the debts owed by the medical school to the vicarious charity of local philanthropists. It was a cold place, with nothing human in its architecture or in its administration.

The little man had decided to start in the basement. This was obvious from the way everyone followed him down the marble stairs at the side of the great entrance hall. Christine had not heard a word of his so far but she gathered, from the comments passed along the line, that in the basement they kept the bodies for dissection. She went down the stairs feeling sick, determined not to look if the bodies could be seen. She had visions of corpses floating face upwards in vats of preserving chemicals, parts of them already decomposed. But the bodies were invisible. In fact there was no proof that they were actually there. All that could be seen were large closed aluminium tanks. The man said that the bodies were kept in these tanks and that whenever a new body was required a porter was sent down to fish one out with a large net on the end of a pole. The students found the notion amusing and much fear and tension was released in their laughter.

Back up the stairs to the museum with Christine and Arthur still at the back of the line. Christine did not like the way their guide was talking about human bodies as if they were objects of fun. Perhaps, as a doctor, he was so used to them that he had no respect for them any more. He was still chattering away when she got to the top of the stairs, saying how the students had been known to play football with the heads of the corpses they were dissecting. They could not afford to take their work too seriously; their seeming disrespect was a psychological defence mechanism to protect them from the horror and distaste vested in the human corpse in our society. At this Flagg nodded his head in agreement.

Good stuff this tour. Psychology in action. These statements would have little weight if they had been recorded in a book or a lecture. They would have been treated with contempt, like the picture of the two babies crying in the first chapter of her psychology textbook. The caption explained that their behaviour was an example of identical twins behaving identically. On to the museum to see heredity at work.

The museum was like any other museum except that the exhibits were human bodies or parts of human bodies. Because this was a medical museum the exhibits were of interest only because they represented perfect examples of humanity at its ugliest; diseased, ravaged by bacteria, malformed at birth, swollen with bulbous cysts and elephantitis. The larger items were in long glass cases in the middle of the room, the smaller and more portable organs hung clinically on the walls. One could see anything from a diseased leg to a complete body, horrible beyond fiction. There was so much to be afraid of in the museum that the laughter had to stop, so much of the 'there but for the grace of God go I' realization that no joke was possible. The medical man journeyed from one glass case to another, explaining the causes and effects of the diseases portrayed, following the purple stains in the veins and arteries with a narrow clinical baton. In general the diseased organs had two colours; grey and purple. The grey was for death and the purple for the benefit of students.

The students listened to his monologue in abject silence, too overcome with the gravity of the exhibition to absorb the information he was giving out. Some of them, Christine included, looked at the floor throughout the address, convinced that they should never have come to this awful place.

P

But there was more to come, another room which they must enter and examine. Heredity was the subject under discussion so they must look at heredity in action. They must examine the exhibits carefully preserved for them by the medical school so that their education in child psychology could be based on real and distasteful fact. The Baby Room it was called. Every item in it had to do with the process of procreation and birth.

The prize exhibits were freaks which had died at birth. One had two heads; another was a cyclops with one eye in the middle of its wide forehead; a third was a perfect monkey with hair all over its body and born, the guide assured them, from a woman who was bald. There was even a twin, extracted from the ovary of its sister twenty years after it should have been born. It had a name – dermoid cyst – together with teeth and hair all bundled up together into a shape the size of a cricket ball. It was not clear whether it was human or malignant growth. Lodged in its sister's ovary, it had begun to grow when the sister conceived a child of her own. The medical man said that it would certainly have killed the sister's baby and maybe the sister into the bargain. Lucky they were able to remove it in time.

It lay, stained and ugly, in its own special case, defying classification.

Christine could not look at any of the exhibits. She found a chair in a corner of the room and she sat down, her head buried in her hands, with the drone of the clinical voice enveloping her in fear and horror. There was a pain in her belly. It was like a period pain but more sharp and more penetrating.

Desperately she tried to cut herself off from that voice. Everything around her reminded her of the hell she must endure because of her folly with Tumble. The foetuses in the glass cases were the monster in her belly crying and screaming for the expiation of her sin. Conceived in sorrow, born in pain, destined for a life of ugliness and misery. High on his throne Satan exalted sat, how one wonders what he's at, smiling in welcome; come to me all you that labour, pale warriors, death pale were they all. Increase and multiply and fill the earth. The child leaped in her womb, leaped with joy.

The pain was greater now. Sharp stabs of knives inside her stomach. She put her head between her knees to bring the blood back to her head and stop herself from fainting, as her father had taught her when he had felt sick in church. Hammers thumped in her ears; blood, blood, jumping up and down. There was a hand on her shoulder, a distant voice in her nightmare.

'Are you feeling ill?' Arthur, kind Arthur. She nodded her head, low down beside her ankles.

'I'll take you home.'

He went away. The pain was leaving too, deadening itself like a headache after aspirin. Slowly, she lifted her head, rested it on the back of the chair. The other students looked at her in sympathy. There, but for the grace of God were they. She tried to smile at them, tried to assure them that she was quite well, that they should ignore her and get on with their work. But her face was ashen, grey with the weeks of isolation in Tumble's flat, and the nausea turbulent within her.

Arthur came back to take her to his car. He took hold of her arm, leading her out of the Baby Room to the entrance hall where he had asked the porter to get her a glass of water.

'You'll be all right, love,' said the porter.

Christine drank the water and thanked the porter for his kindness.

'You'd better get her home, sir. Her face is a bad colour.'

Arthur helped her into his car, strapping her carefully into her safety belt. While they were driving through the university precinct the pain began again, coming at her in storms and bursts, bending her double across the safety belt. She vomited a little on the floor of the car.

She was able to let herself into Tumble's flat. Arthur wanted to stay with her for a while to make sure that she was all right. He wanted to call her doctor, because he did not understand why she should have such a pain. But she made him go away, telling him that the pain was only her period, that this happened every month and that all she had to do was to go to bed with a hot water bottle held tightly to her stomach and it would go away.

After he left she went to the bathroom where she vomited again, this time so fiercely that she thought her whole stomach would be thrown up. Then the agony began to burn. Shafts of terror pierced her loins, movements, stirrings in her womb. It seemed that the Black Plague was in her stomach, tearing at her flesh with teeth as sharp as rats' eyes.

It was over sooner than she had expected. It seemed as if all of her had suffered in the release of her child, as if every part of her body had to absorb the anguish of its struggles to survive. But it had died, and in dying it might have solved the problems of the nightmare. In a sense it did.

Totally senseless with the pain, Christine left the bathroom to go into the kitchen where she put her head into the gas oven and went to sleep.

Later, when the gas reached the pilot light, there was a terrific explosion. Its force carried Christine's body to the other end of the kitchen, severing her head from her trunk on the corner of the stainless steel sink.

The head fell into Tumble's great plant pot, a detail which did not escape the notice of a cub reporter from the local paper, who was able to reveal to the world that he, too, was a scholar. His headline read 'The Basil Pot Suicide'.

Benediction

Joachim did not read the newspapers any more. He remained ignorant, therefore, of the tragedy of Christine's death until he went into the department of Sociology and Social Administration three weeks after it had happened. By then, of course, his sense of horror was untimely. The other members of staff had grown accustomed to the macabre details and had become more interested in those consequences of Christine's death which could be seen in the shifts and shufflings of relationships and power in the department.

Joachim's visit was not accidental; he did not go to pay a social visit or to see his friends. The only reason he left his room that morning was that he had received a summons from Professor Warble asking him to present himself for interview. There was to be a meeting to discuss his future in the department. That, Joachim assumed, reasonably, meant the sack.

For the past five months he had received a monthly salary for doing precisely nothing. The fact that he had done nothing was not his fault; he was working under Tumble and Tumble had asked him to wait for instructions. But, since Christmas, he had not even waited for instructions. He hadn't even gone to work. No employer, however enlightened, could be expected to tolerate that level of productivity. They would probably pay him until the end of the academic year by which time he would be expected to have found another job.

He dressed slowly that morning. He had not been out of the house for so long that he had almost forgotten what it felt like to wear a fresh shirt and a good suit. His razor blade had exhausted all the nine lives it was reputed to possess but he used it all the same, taking his time, stroking his chin carefully and painfully. His face was grey with being in the house too long, his hair thick and oily because he had not washed it.

After he had shaved he took off his pyjama trousers and climbed into the bath, which had been filling while he had been looking at himself in the shaving mirror. In the bath he washed himself indolently, every part of him carelessly soaped and rinsed in a narcissistic ritual of purification in preparation for the sacrifice. A thick grey scum floated on the bath water while he lay back after his labours. He spent ten minutes watching it, wondering how he was going to get out of the bath without covering himself in the slime he had just washed from his body.

He walked, naked, into his room. There was no one to see his nakedness, no one to scream in horror or swoon in passion at the sight of his young clean body.

His shirt felt good, so good in fact that he wondered why he had not bathed and put it on before. It would have cheered him up during his depression. By the time he was fully dressed he was definitely a new man; as he brushed his suit he was smiling.

He walked to the university in the sunlight. There were no traces of the snow which had upset the city for so long. There had been some rain while he was in the bathroom. Not much rain, just enough to dampen the grass in the square and to darken the colour of the barren soil on the bomb site. The streets were drying under the pale sun as he walked along them. It was a lovely day to lose a job on, he mused.

He went first to the room he shared with Gerry and Nick Hill, wondering whether Pentup Emotion had, in fact, disappeared as Gerry had suggested in his letter. Gerry and Nick Hill were at their desks when he walked into the room. Neither seemed particularly busy.

'Hi, Kim. How's your scene been?' Nick Hill was sitting back on his chair, the front legs raised off the ground, his own feet planted on his desk between his adding machine and his card index system.

'Good morning, men.' Joachim smiled at Gerry and then at Nick Hill. Gerry said nothing.

'How is everything here? I see Pentup's still missing.' Joachim asked Gerry but the reply came from Nick Hill.

'Revolutions, man. Tumble rumbled in a pretty *coup d'état* which sent Charles to the top of the class.'

'What is he talking about?' Joachim looked to Gerry again, this time for a translation. Gerry was slow to speak. It was obvious that he did not know where to start.

'It's so long since we've seen you that I don't know where to begin. I don't know how much you know already.'

'I know nothing. Start at the beginning.' Joachim sat down at his desk which was covered in circulars and notices of functions, dances, debates and exhibitions taking place in the university buildings during the spring term. He swept them into the waste paper basket and waited, with a clean desk, to listen to what Gerry had to say.

'Well. You know that they have created a new chair in Sociological Research and that Tumble was hot favourite for it?'

'That I knew. You told me in your letter.'

'Well, he didn't get it.'

'Who did?'

'Charles Pretty.'

'But he doesn't know the first thing about Sociology or research. He's a philosopher.'

'Everyone knows that. But they had to give it to somebody and they obviously couldn't give it to Tumble.'

'Why not?'

Gerry looked at Joachim. So he hadn't heard yet about Christine's suicide. That must be why he hadn't said anything about it when he came in.

'You have been locked away. Don't you read the papers?'

'Not since Vicky died. Why? Has Tumble been up to something?'

'The girl he was living with committed suicide. She was a student here so they couldn't make him a prof. after that.'

'Poor devil.'

'Picture in all the papers, man. Object of the nation's wrath. Took the role over when you put it down.' Nick Hill supplied more details.

'I see,' said Joachim thoughtfully. He sympathized with Tumble. Those Pressmen must have made a feast out of the affair. Lecturer at university living in sin with student who commits suicide. He didn't have to read the papers to know what they said about that.

'Why did the girl commit suicide?'

'She'd just had a miscarriage. The coroner said that the balance of her mind was definitely disturbed. Said it had nothing to do with Tumble, who was here when she did it. Tumble said he wanted to marry her but she wouldn't have him.'

'Poor devil,' Joachim said again. 'Who was the girl? Did you know her?'

This was the part Gerry had avoided since he had been forced to tell the story. Still Joachim would have to find out sooner or later.

'It was Christine Murray.'

'Who?'

'Christine. The girl you took out last term.'

'No!'

'I'm afraid so.'

'I can't believe it.' It was true. He could not believe it. Christine dead. Christine committing suicide because she had had a miscarriage. Impossible. It was too sordid. She was not like that at all. Why she was as virginal as a new-born baby. How the hell could she have got mixed up in that sort of situation?

'As soon as the news broke, Charles Pretty started a campaign to get rid of Tumble. Openly condemned him in the common room. Accused him of murder. There was a terrible row. Everyone watched them fighting but Pretty had right on his side so Tumble had to run away with his tail between his legs.'

Joachim did not hear what Gerry was saying. He was trying to work out how Christine could have come to be pregnant and dead in such a short time. Tumble must have been the man who got her pregnant otherwise she would not have gone to live with him. How the hell had the bastard seduced her?

'Where is he?' Joachim got up from his chair. It was obvious to Gerry that his early sympathy for Tumble's predicament had been replaced by condemnation.

'Sit down, Joachim. He's gone away. Nobody knows where he is.'

'He lives in a flat in that park by the river, doesn't he? I'll break his bloody neck.' Joachim moved to the door. His hand was on the handle and he was turning it much farther than it was supposed to be turned. He was so angry he felt he could have ripped the door down with one hand.

'Sit down, Joachim,' Gerry said again. 'He's moved out of there. He moved out of there as soon as it happened. Everyone thinks he's gone down to London.'

Joachim let go of the door handle. He walked over to the window and looked out. If Christine had allowed Tumble to seduce her had she done so because he had rejected her? Could he have some responsibility for her death? This was why he wanted to find Tumble. This was why he wanted to beat the brains out of Tumble. Because he was afraid that he himself might have had some part in Christine's suicide and he did not want to believe it.

The phone in the room rang briefly. Nick Hill answered it. He always answered the phone. He had put it on his desk so that he could make calls without having to move too far from his machinery.

'Right,' was all he said to the caller and then he put the phone down.

'They want you.' He reported to Joachim, who was not listening.

'Warble wants you now, man.'

Joachim left the room without saying anything to the other two. When he reached Warble's office his mind was far away from the interview. He knocked and was instructed to enter.

There were three men in Warble's office; Padd, Pretty and Warble himself. They were seated in a semicircle and there was an empty chair in front of them which was meant for Joachim.

'Come in and sit down, Ryan. I hope you are feeling better now. We all shared your grief when that terrible thing happened to your housekeeper.'

What the hell was the man talking about? Housekeeper. He had never had a housekeeper in his life. Was he talking about Vicky?

'Thank you. It was something of a shock.' The words came out of his mouth but they were the words and sentiments of a man he did not know.

'I must say that we did not know that you lived in such a colourful household. We were all very impressed, not with the tragic murder, of course, but with the fact that you had gone to live there in the first place. That's the only way to do research in sociology. Go out and live among the people. Are you interested in prostitution?'

Interested in Prostitution. Sociological research. What had they got to do with Vicky's murder? Or Christine's for that matter?

'No. Not any more.' Again the foreigner spoke, using his mouth and his accents.

'Yes. I think we understand your sentiments.' Warble looked at his two colleagues who nodded wisely.

'Well, Ryan. What we have to say to you is both good news and bad news. I think we'll give you the bad news first. You know that the research project on which you were recruited has now folded up which means that we no longer require your services as a Research assistant.' Warble paused here, to let the bad news sink in.

'But before you grow too pessimistic I must tell you that we do not intend to dispense with your services altogether. You must also know that Quentin Tumble has left us.' Again there was a short pause, a silence of condemnation.

'His departure means that we must fill his post and we propose to offer that post to you.'

'To me?' The foreigner spoke through Joachim again, saying the right thing at the right time.

'Yes, Ryan. To you. Pretty has convinced Padd and myself that you are a gifted young man, that you were not used properly by Tumble and that you should be given the opportunity to show what you can do in a real way, by doing a man's job. You will not have Tumble's status, of course. The appointment will be at lecturer level.'

'Thank you very much.'

'So you accept then?'

'Of course.' The foreigner accepted. Joachim was still thinking about Christine and how impossible it was that she could be dead.

'Well. That's settled. Close the door on your way out, please, Ryan. We have several things to discuss before the next interview.'

Joachim walked out of the room, taking the foreigner with him. His first thought was to go for a drink. Out of the building and into the pub to see whether he could find real people there.

The world had gone mad today. Promotion and death. Guilt and reward. Nothing fitted into a pattern any more. He ordered a large whisky. When it came it tasted like whisky, scalding his throat as he drank it. So far it was the only real thing which had happened to him that day. You're getting drunk, the foreigner whispered in his ear.

'If you can't think of anything sensible to say then you might as well shut up.'

He ordered another whisky at the bar. When the barman

brought it he asked if Joachim would like some soda. Joachim thanked him kindly but declined his offer. The only thing he trusted was the whisky. The soda might be like everything else he had tasted this morning.

'You should really have soda. And something to eat,' said the foreigner.

Joachim drank the whisky in one gulp. It burned his throat but he was prepared to suffer any torture if by suffering he could spite the foreigner.

'Another one, please,' he called out to the barman, 'and a pint of bitter.'

There was a seat in the corner of the room. It was just below a window which looked out on to the street. He thought it might be pleasant to sit by that window so he took his beer and whisky over there, setting it down carefully on a table. He was unable to let his mind settle on any of the daft things which had happened in the department. His normal practice when he had problems of guilt was to examine his conduct in the manner laid down in the catechism and to see if there was a chance that he was not responsible for this or that particular action. But there was so much to think about. So much to rationalize in the Christine Murray part of his life that he couldn't settle on that.

How was it that the university could kick out Tumble for living with a student and promote him when he was nationally recognized as a man who cohabited with prostitutes? How could they promote him when he had not done a day's work for them since he had joined them? Where was the logic? Or, if there was no logic, where was the vested interest?

Gerry came into the pub as he was finishing his beer. He saw Joachim in the corner and he came over at once.

'Hello, Joachim. Is everything all right?'

'Everything is crazy. They have given me Tumble's job.'

'Congratulations. What will you have to celebrate?'

'I shall have a large whisky and a pint of beer.'

You're a fool said the foreigner, you should have something to eat.

Gerry seemed relieved to find Joachim. He had obviously come into the pub to find him though he did not say why. Perhaps he was afraid that Joachim, whom he would expect to feel some responsibility for Christine's suicide, might do something silly himself. He was happy to find the man getting drunk.

'I can't stay very long,' he said when he came back with the drinks. 'I have an interview with Warble this afternoon.'

'Perhaps they will promote you too.'

'Not a chance. I have decided to leave the university. I have got myself a teaching job in a London comprehensive school and while I'm down there I shall look for the mandarins.'

'You won't find them in a comprehensive school.'

Gerry refused Joachim's offer of a drink. He left as soon as he finished his half of bitter. Joachim got himself another pint and another whisky and when he had finished them he knew that he was drunk.

You should have had something to eat, said the foreigner.

Joachim began the walk home. The sun seemed stronger now than it had been when he had left the house. It made him feel rather mad.

There was a wall near the pavement on which he was walking. It separated the pavement from a hospital and he thought he would like to walk along that wall so he climbed up and walked along it, six feet taller than all the other pedestrians going his way.

Get down, said the foreigner, you're behaving like a child.

Joachim got down from the wall by way of a lampstandard which stood about four feet from it. He slid down the lampstandard and then he did a sort of maypole dance around it.

You're making a spectacle of yourself, said the foreigner. The best thing you can do is go back home and lie down.

Joachim thought he might enjoy frightening the other pedestrians if he could find a hedge or something and leap out at them as they went past. There was no hedge, of course, but here were lots of doorways, the most suitable being the door of a public Gents which he wanted to visit anyway. So he tried that a few times, leaping out of the Gents at shoppers and housewives, scaring the pants off them with his funny faces and his screams. He gave up when an old woman dropped a dozen eggs on the pavement and the foreigner got the better of him.

They'll get a policeman, said the foreigner.

He had to cross the road to get to his flat. He waited for the traffic to allow him to cross and while he waited he had an idea. There was only one way to cross a road in these troubled times: by forward roll. He had been good at forward rolls. Stand up straight, feet together and then fall forward, kicking off to give sufficient momentum to keep the turn. He rolled across the road, enjoying it so much that he rolled back again.

It's silly and dangerous doing forward rolls in the road. Why don't you try the grass over there?

'That's the first sensible thing you've said.'

Joachim rolled over to the grass. To get to it he had to cross the road, travel along twenty yards of pavement and then go through the gate into the square where the grass was waiting for him. He completed his journey without a pause, performing rolls of great beauty and simplicity.

He rolled around the square. Over and over and over without ever stopping to rest or to congratulate himself. While he rolled children stopped their games and began to watch him. They were joined by pedestrians and other passers-by. People left their bus-stops to come over to see what he was doing and what he was doing was rolling over and over and over.

Soon a great circle of spectators gathered round the square, watching him in silence, waiting for him to get his camel through the eye of his needle.